MURDER BY DEADLINE

MURDER BY DEADLINE

•

Mel Taylor

AVALON BOOKS
NEW YORK

Published by Thomas Bouregy & Co., Inc.
160 Madison Avenue, New York, NY 10016

Library of Congress Cataloging-in-Publication Data

Taylor, Mel.
    Murder by deadline / Mel Taylor.
        p. cm.
    ISBN 0-8034-9748-2 (acid-free paper)
    1. Journalists—Fiction. 2. Florida—Fiction. I. Title.

    PS3570.A9462M87 2005
    813'.6—dc22

                                    2005011193

PRINTED IN THE UNITED STATES OF AMERICA
ON ACID-FREE PAPER
BY HADDON CRAFTSMEN, BLOOMSBURG, PENNSYLVANIA

To Aron and Kathleen

acknowledgments

I want to thank the talented members of the Thursday Group. Their support and guidance helped me tremendously. The group was started by author Joyce Sweeney, a friend and teacher.

I also want to thank Carol Cope for being a good listener and Rich Babl for pointing me in the right direction in the beginning. On the technical end, I owe thanks to Norman Kassoff and Bob White. I am grateful to Assistant Editor Orly Trieber at Avalon Books for her valuable input.

South Florida is home to many great mystery writers. I have been fortunate to be able to draw upon their wisdom.

Chapter One

"This is a mistake. I shouldn't have called." Her voice was cautious, the words measured, with a tone of exacerbation. There were thousands of phone calls made to a newsroom. Landlord-tenant disputes or calls from jail inmates claiming innocence. Yet, I didn't want to lose the call.

"If I can help you, then it's not a mistake." I pressed the phone closer to my ear, closing off the noise from a bank of televisions to my left.

"I was putting together some information on stalking and I remembered the stories you did last month. And—" I heard a scratching noise, then the sound of the phone clanging on a hard surface. The voice came back a few seconds later. "Skids, stop it."

"Skids?"

"Just my cat. Sorry, I dropped the telephone. She walks on everything and tries to play with my phone. She thinks it's a toy."

I paused. "Is someone following you?"

Silence. Five, then ten seconds passed.

"No bother," I said. "I was just asking. Is it okay if I get your name?"

"Like I said, I think it was a mistake to call. I really don't want to get into this on the phone. Thanks."

"But if there's a problem, you should get some help."

A pause. "I don't want to make a big deal out of this, but someone . . . it's probably nothing."

"That's what I'm here for. You say someone?"

"I really should go."

"You sure?"

"I'm sure."

"I like the name of your cat."

"Skids?"

"If you want to call back, I get in early. The name is Matt Bowens."

"Matt!" The yell came from Ike Cashing who was standing in the middle of the room. "We've got one minute! I need you in front on the camera." Ike flipped a switch and the studio lights lit up the room like daylight. He aimed his camera at an empty chair. "C'mon man, get off that phone," Ike urged.

"Look, you don't have to give me a name," I told her. "But I want you to call me if you're in any trouble."

"It's nothing. Really, it's probably nothing. I just wanted the information. Thanks for your help. Good-bye." There was a certain grace in her voice, leaving me with a void, knowing she may not call back.

"Matt," Ike said.

I eased the phone down and stepped over dangling cables from the camera which lined the floor like so much black spaghetti. I picked up the microphone, clipped it to my tie, jammed my earpiece into place, sat down, and looked into the lens. A voice flowed through the earpiece.

"So you decided to join us for some television, eh Matt?" Courtney Rolund, the six o'clock producer was twenty-five miles away in Miami. But the clarity of the earpiece gave me the impression she was standing right there in my face.

"Thirty seconds to your piece Matt." Her low, even voice had a salty smoothness. Then: "Tell Ike to rebalance the camera. The coloring is way off."

I checked the in-house monitor. Only television could make a black man green. I held up my writing pad. Ike zoomed in on the white piece of paper to let the camera realign its memory for all the colors in the universe.

"We're coming to you in fifteen seconds," she said. "Tell him to zoom out!"

I repeated the command to Ike and waited. My script was committed to memory, but lingering questions about the woman on the phone distracted me. Ike clicked the controls, zooming the picture and framing into position. I could hear the anchors in Miami through the earpiece.

"Reporter Matt Bowens has more. He's in Fort Lauderdale. Matt . . ."

For about forty seconds, I told south Florida about a rip-off scam involving an elderly couple. Two men claimed their roof needed repairs. Eleven thousand dollars and three weeks later, the thugs failed to show up for work. When the taped portion of my report ended, I wrapped it up with tips on how to spot a con game, and threw it back to the news anchors in Miami.

Ike dragged his right hand against the wall switch. The stark white television lights powered down. "That was close. Who was that on the phone, the president?"

"Just someone looking for help," I told him.

Mike Brendon, the assignment editor, waved me over to his desk. My steps took me past the gleaming yellow Channel 14 logo on the wall, and a huge window, with a view of Biscayne Bay. Dozens of boats were lined up in the slips, their tall masts rising out of the blue-black water. A few miles off, a collection of clouds bunched up over the Atlantic, lightning etched against the sky, thunder backfiring in the distance.

"You know Ramirez is going to be here in the morning." Brendon took his gaze away from the wall of televisions. "He needs to see you before you go out."

Mike pushed the remnants of the day, personal calendar, and notes into a briefcase as he talked. "Seems you're in line for some big project. He won't even tell me about it."

I heard Ike in the background unsnapping the camera from the tripod, and the clatter of equipment being packed away.

Ike's gear revealed the nicks of more than twenty years in

news. There was the gouge in the tripod from a bullet graze from a gun-in-the-air reveler while videotaping a New Year's Eve celebration. A trial defendant pushed Ike to the ground, leaving a four-inch gash on the camera housing. Scratches and bumps from thousands of encounters, and stakeouts.

Ike stopped his movement when Brendon spoke about a special project as if to see if he was involved. The last time the news director came up to Fort Lauderdale for any reason, a deadline loomed to renew my contract. But that was finished and signed three months ago. The main studio and most of the staff were stationed in Miami.

I tried to read Mike's face to get a hint of what Ramirez would tell me. "What time is he coming?"

"He'll be up before noon. Now, if you don't mind, I've got to get in one last meal." Brendon pushed his two-hundred-and-sixty-plus pounds from the chair.

"He was thinking about creating a new position," Brendon added. "Maybe that's it?"

"What are you getting ready for?" I asked.

"A diet." His lips rippled a sliver of movement. The words rolled out in marked tones of dejection. "See this?" Brendon jammed two plump hands into his sides.

"My cholesterol is way up, and the doc says I'm eighty pounds too much. I'm being ordered." His voice dragged again.

Brendon was nowhere near my six-foot-two-inch frame.

"You've got to start this diet tomorrow?"

His head bobbled a strained yes, like a doomed man. He slid a right hand down a crimson beard, stopping at the tip, then repeated the move a few times, until he paused to push the glasses back on his nose.

"Good luck," I said.

Brendon pulled the briefcase to his side. "I'm going to eat myself into the size of a refrigerator by morning. Then I'll be ready."

We stepped through the doorway to leave, yet still listening for chatter on the police scanners. Brendon eased the key from his pocket. A Monday night police blotter could fill with reasons to pull us back into the newsroom. Stabbings, overturned cars on the highway, a child found wandering the streets. But there was nothing. A rare moment of quiet in south Florida. We left in different directions.

I stretched my fingers around the wheel of the BMW. The new-car smell was gone, long replaced by the scent of brine-soaked sand and road dust. I sat behind the wheel with thoughts of the phone call. But three people were waiting for me. I slid the gear into drive, and rolled out into traffic.

Chapter Two

The music was so loud, I could hear Marvin Gaye as soon as I stopped and cracked the door of the Beemer. Front and side windows to the stucco house were open to catch a surge of evening coolness. No one answered my first series of knocks, so I kept my finger on the bell until the music dropped in volume. The knob turned and the door jerked open.

"Matt, get in here. You've got to help us settle a bet." Cat Miller grabbed my arm and pulled me into the living room, close to the epicenter of Marvin's prescription.

And when I get that feeling, I want sexual healing.

The confident spirit in Cat was a factor, but it wasn't the core of what drove me to her. Her eyes did. They were hazel, exotic as a sunset, against cheeks of dark brown, skin as smooth as Blackstrap molasses. She got the nickname from her father and rarely used Yvonne. After her mother's death, she gave Cat the south Florida home. Cat traced her hand down the side of my arm, sliding her fingers into mine.

"You've got to do this for me," she whispered.

"Do what? I thought we were going out for dinner?"

"A friend just moved down. Follow me." She squeezed my left hand, and guided me toward a circular glass table.

"Stacy, this is Matt Bowens."

A hand of fingers, all pencil thin, reached up to shake. A collection of bracelets rattled as she drew her hand back. I underestimated her strength. She had a firm grip. Her hair was pulled back in a clasp. The dress was business length and her smile was cordial.

"Hi Matt. I'm Stacy Gaines. I met Cat years ago at Atlanta University."

"It wasn't *that* many years ago!" Cat shouted.

"Well, it was before gray became your second hair color!" Stacy cracked back.

Cat yanked her right hand from me and stroked the two or three gray hairs in a field of black, and smoothed them to the back with a long stroke. "You're the one who probably gave me those grays."

Cat never finished college, preoccupied with a failed marriage and two children. "Enough about my hair." Cat angled her head at me. "Answer a question Matt. Where did we first meet?"

"That's easy. The bar and grill just down the street from the station. The one with three levels. I nearly knocked you down the stairway when I bumped into you."

Cat smiled the look of a winner.

"All right Matt," Stacy challenged, "where did you go on your first date?"

My jaw dropped just enough to show my top row of teeth. The words wouldn't come. My mind ricocheted through all the restaurants, clubs, and late-evening flirtations. What if I said the wrong thing? I froze for a moment and leaned back a bit to let Marvin's singing fill in the cavernous gap.

Wake up! Wake up! Wake up! Wake up! 'Cause you do it right!

Stacy aimed a gold-tipped fingernail at me. "See! I told you he wouldn't remember."

"The Brass Stump," I blurted. "We ate dinner at the Brass Stump down by Riverwalk."

Stacy frowned. "Some men can't remember."

"Don't go betting against Matt." Cat beamed.

I felt uncomfortable being the subject of conversation and I was afraid of what game question would be next. I needed the support of another male, even if he was only four years old.

"Where's the kids?" I asked.

Cat cocked her head toward the back door. "Tell them we're going to order pizza."

"I can't stay," Stacy said. "I've got work to do." Her walnut-brown eyes ping-ponged between me and Cat. I eased away from the table. Cat shadowed my steps to the back door. I stepped onto the patio and felt Cat's arm wrap around my waist. She closed the sliding glass door behind us, leaving Stacy watching our movements. Cat's tongue flicked at my left earlobe, triggering surges pulsing through every nerve cell. I was about to look back into her eyes but her grip on my waist started to feel more like an anaconda's fatal hug. There was anger in her grasp. The tongue jerked away from me, shocking my ear with a sudden sensation of cold air.

"That wasn't where we went." Cat's words were so soft I had a hard time hearing them. But she had my attention. "There was no way I was going to let Stacy say she was right. Now who did you *really* take to the Brass Stump?"

"It was a mistake . . . I remember now. We ate at The Landscape, over on Stirling Road. There's so many restaurants!"

I paused to see if I had the right answer.

"Okay. You finally got the place right."

I turned to meet her eyes, which set off thoughts about that night we met. I had settled in at the second-floor bar, with a glass of white zinfandel and three friends, all of us mounted on bar stools. The wine demanded a second sip until Yvonne Cat Miller walked by. Our meeting was almost a year ago.

"What are you talking about?" The question came from Jason, the preschooler. He stood a few feet from us, armed with a laser tag gun in one hand and a big-splash squirt gun slung over his small shoulder.

Cat released her arm from around me. She stepped back and grabbed the handle of the door. "Matt can explain. Can't you Matt?" I watched Cat's smirk through the glass slider as she closed it back into position.

My years growing up in a Chicago housing project, escaping street gangs, surviving a gunshot, four years of college, and another twelve covering news stories, did not prepare me for a four-year-old. I knew there would be interesting moments dating the single mother of two children. Most of the time, I answered all of Jason's questions. This time, a second option seemed best. I changed the subject.

"How far does that gun squirt water?" I asked, waiting to see if I could knock him off his concentration.

"Far. See."

He slid the green plastic weapon down from his shoulder. A tiny trigger finger flashed, and streams of water cascaded over an empty cardboard box.

"Hey! Stop that!" Shauna, age eight, popped up from behind the box. "You're getting me all wet! Go back inside Jason!"

The youngster shook his head and body in an emphatic no.

"He's not going back in there because he's been bad," Shauna volunteered.

"What did you do Jason?"

The tiny shoulders sagged. His head was bent over his scuffed shoes. I peeked at Shauna, who was eager to give me an answer.

"He doesn't want to go in there because he got into the cake." Shauna stood, arms crossed with the stern look of a prosecutor before a jury. Her right foot tapped the ground with the cadence of a child's heartbeat.

Jason aimed his weapon toward Shauna. She slapped her fingers against her head, protecting a round face. Her anxious eyes peered back at me through a mask of hands.

I waited until I got Jason's attention. "I'll tell you what, Jason. Let me help you out, okay?" He lowered the squirt gun.

The sliding glass door opened. Cat stepped out. "Matt, can you give Stacy a ride to the hotel? We've got to wait on the pizza." Cat rolled her eyes from Shauna to Jason. "Is something wrong?"

"No. I can take her now," I said.

"You sure everything's okay?"

Detectives should throw away their lie detectors, I reasoned. All they've got to do is let a mother sit in. Stacy stepped past Cat and yelled to Jason.

"Good-bye angel."

Jason's face crinkled up, confused. Obviously, no one had used that word before to address him. Stacy said good-bye to Shauna and turned back into the kitchen. Jason's eyes followed me inside. Instead of tracking Stacy and Cat through the house, I detoured to the cake. It was sitting on the edge of the counter. Three swipes, each the width of a child's finger, lined the side of the cake which faced the wall. I dug my index finger into the soft icing until I connected all three lines.

"What are you doing?" Cat demanded.

"Sorry, couldn't wait." I pulled fingers covered in white frosting through my lips.

"Didn't anyone teach you better than that?"

I looked back to see Jason grinning. He dropped his gear and ran after me. Our high-five must have left Cat searching for an answer to our jubilation. I opened the car door for Stacy, let her inside and backed up the Beemer.

I knew rush hour traffic on I-95 was gone, so a trip downtown and back to Cat's neighborhood in the northern part of the county wouldn't take too long. The music of Marvin Gaye still hummed inside my head until Stacy started tossing questions at me like darts.

"Are you and Cat serious?"

"Let's just say we're not seeing anyone else right now."

She lobbed another one. "So, is there talk of marriage here?"

"You ask some personal questions for someone I've just met."

"Maybe *we've* just met, but I've known Cat for a long time. And after that whole thing with her former husband—"

She turned toward the window and the cars passing us on Sample Road. "So you don't mind dating a single mother of two, when you can date—"

"I can understand your concern. I know all about her ex. I know how he treated her and his time in jail, but I have to be honest, we haven't talked about that subject."

Another dart. "So you're not serious?"

I didn't answer.

"I'm sorry Matt, it's just that I don't want her to go through some nightmare. Not again. Although she wrote me about you."

"And?"

"It was all good. Says you're especially good with the kids. And for Cat, that's important."

"Anything else?"

"Well, she told me when you were a teenager, you were shot."

The steering wheel brushed through my fingers as I moved two lanes to the right and straightened up the ride. The memory of being shot sent tendrils of pain shooting through my chest, stopping at the scar tissue three inches to the right of my heart. The bullet passed through me. A slow simmer boiled within me. Stacy probably knew a great deal about me, and she was still a stranger.

"Why did you come down? A job?" I asked.

"There's a new position which opened up. I'm sorry but I can't talk about it much. But yes, if it all goes well, it will be a great new step for me."

It was my turn to play darts.

"What company?"

"Can't say."

"Some place downtown?"

"I said . . . I can't talk about it."

"Is it okay if I ask *you* a personal question?" I kept my eyes forward. The BMW sped up the ramp and bolted into southbound expressway traffic.

"Maybe," she said.

"Who are you running from?"

Bullseye.

The small laugh under her breath made me turn toward her for the length of a glance. Her chest swelled and deflated with a deep sigh before she answered. "Can't fool you, can I?"

The evening sky was a patchwork of dirt gray clouds turning into an orange sunset. Cars heading north on I-95 cast light beams. Stacy never withdrew her stare from the dashboard. "My boyfriend didn't want me to come down here. But the opportunity was too great."

I dropped the questions and fought back a reporter's curiosity about her prospective job. The information would come in time. In my rearview mirror, cars trailed, then passed me. A cab pulled along my window. The driver seemed to take time to look into my BMW. But then it was getting dark and faces became part of the blur of driving. I turned onto Broward Boulevard. We reached the hotel minutes later.

"Thanks for the ride," Stacy said.

I nodded. "Thanks for looking out for Cat."

She waved and yelled back. "By the way, my boyfriend couldn't remember anything about our first date." She turned to the lobby. An odd sense moved through me. I stepped out of the car and swiveled my body toward the street traffic. I half expected to greet a face from the past. Someone I hadn't seen in a long time. But no one was there. Just the cars forming lines in front of the red light.

Chapter Three

I walked in the direction of the Channel 14 building, but stopped when Mike Brendon pushed open the tinted-glass door to greet me. His left cheek bulged to the size of a golf ball. He spoke through the chews.

"I'll take your briefcase . . . got to send you . . . over to Ranklin Avenue."

He paused, probably, so he wouldn't choke. I was close enough to take in the sweet smell of bacon which scented the air until a January breeze whisked the aroma toward downtown Fort Lauderdale.

"And what's there?" I pulled out my reporter pad and watched a slight movement in his throat.

"We've got a signal five. Someone found a body in a field. Can't tell you much else. Ike is pulling the car around." Brendon reached for my briefcase. He raised the sandwich in the air like some miracle cure. "My diet."

The door closed behind him as he got out the last few words. Ike's news van eased to a slow roll. It kept moving forward and never came to a full stop. I cradled into the seat as Ike crunched the gas pedal. The jolt pushed me back.

"And good morning to you." My words were smothered in sarcasm.

"Don't mind me. I had a bad night." Ike Cashing wrapped both hands around the steering wheel and yanked it downward, making a sharp right onto third Avenue. We headed

south, past the government building which used to be a
Burdines department store. Across the street, the county
environmental office was once a men's clothing shop. And
just blocks away, a post office. Years before it was an A&P
grocery. All recycled buildings. We crossed Broward
Boulevard.

I watched people and faces, marked with confidence,
walk distances from automobile to office. Through dozens
of interviews, I knew they were friendly to a tourist but not
unlike the nine-to-fivers of any large city, they talked about
how crime secured a place in their thoughts. They stepped
with a certain purpose, the same steadfastness they brought
with them from New York, Philadelphia, and like Ike
Cashing, from the Midwest. Just faces looking to start over.
Ike once referred to himself as having a recycled life.

We left the downtown area. I waited for Ike to tell me
about his rough night. He stayed silent and I gave up when
we turned onto Ranklin Avenue. Three police cars and a
crime scene van took up most of the block. We parked. I
approached the field, which connected two subdivisions.
The undeveloped land, in dire need of mowing, was a distance from any house. Ike reached for his camera.

Frank Walker, the police spokesman, was already there.
He stepped in front of me before I reached the yellow crime
tape. Both his hands were up, palms facing me in a
don't-take-another-step stance.

"You can move up to the tape and take your pictures if
you want, but . . ." There was a firmness in his voice.

I looked past Walker. About fifty feet from me, the wind
whipped the leaves of a southern maple tree. Two detectives
stood near the tree trunk. A third stepped a slow pace, yards
away, looking down at the ground as he walked. A crime
tech raised his camera. The flash matched the brilliance of
the Tuesday morning sunlight. He aimed again and took
another picture. Then he aimed a second camera, a digital
one, and captured the image. The breeze caught the collar of
his jacket, sending the corners upward toward his ears. He
folded the collar back into position and moved to his right.

Then I saw her. One arm was fully extended over her head with her hand touching the ground. The other, somewhere beneath her prone body. She wore a blue knee-length skirt that was lined with dirt, and matching jacket, open to a white blouse. The loose strands of her brown hair kicked up with the gust. Now I understood why Walker wanted me to wait. Her head was angled so her face pointed directly at us, bleach-white and rigid. Her eyes were open, their glow gone in the darkening moments after death. Yet, each one was so clear, they could have been the eyes of a mannequin.

I stood next to Walker. Behind me, I heard palm fronds slapping together in the sweeping air. Her right cheek, pink from blood settling in one area, rested on a mound of dollar weed. A teardrop of faded red dripped from her nose, much smaller than the brick-sized blood stain covering her blouse. One shoe was missing. I looked for it among the soda cans and shards of broken glass.

Ike's jostling with the camera cut through the quiet. Crime victims, exposed and uncovered, were never shown on our newscasts. He kept the camera pointed down and waited. A detective covered the body with a tarp.

Only then, I felt I could pull my gaze away from her. Take the image and secure it away. Separate emotion from clear objectivity. Just keep thinking that the emotional scars will never surface. But I know they will, when reporters talk about the tragedies they have seen. I've seen my share: The tears of a murder victim's family, huddled together in a courtroom when a verdict was read. The screeching wails of a woman after getting the whispered word from police about a baby killed in a traffic accident. A man walking down the street clutching a severed head wrapped in a paper bag. A cleanup crew, clad in boots and masks, assigned to wash down blood and brain matter after a husband attacked his wife with an ax.

Countless bodies carried to the morgue. The smell of death. Moments and horrid images sealed forever in my memory, stacked on top of each other, like some endless pool settling in my core. Now I could add those vacant eyes which kept staring at me.

Ike focused the camera on the tarp. Walker turned to me when I flipped through my pad looking for a blank page. I knew Walker for more than a decade, long before he took on the extra weight and hair loss. His days of chasing down a perp were past him, and he readily accepted the assignment of answering questions from reporters.

"Okay Frank, who found her?"

"A woman out for her walk."

"Is she still here?"

"Naw, she's down at the station. As you can imagine, she wanted to get away from here. She's pretty shook up."

A crime tech moved closer to the arrangement of soda cans and took another photograph.

"Any idea *when* this happened?"

Walker shook his head. "Not exactly. Not until the autopsy, but this happened sometime overnight. It's probably too early, but we're checking with missing persons."

"Any ID?"

"Zilch."

"Rape victim?"

"Matt, you know it's too early to tell on something like that. But I'll tell you . . ." Walker lowered his voice to keep the conversation between us.

"Someone really went at her with something."

Over my shoulder, I heard two, perhaps three other cars. Reporters, and photographers emerged, pulling out tripods and microphones. The horde had arrived.

"Frank, is she wearing a wedding ring?"

"I'll tell you what, let me chat with the detectives and see what they want to release. I'll come back and we'll talk."

Frank stretched the yellow police tape upward, ducking head and body under the plastic.

"What do you think Ike?"

Ike stepped away from the camera, and scanned the area left to right. "Obviously someone dumped her here. But did you see the way she was dressed? Like she was going to some kind of meeting."

Walker turned from the detectives, reaching me in quick

steps, until he stopped at the crime tape. There was a certain urgency in his gait which caused everyone else to close in around me.

"We're working another scene. A car has been located over on Seaview and Ninth Ave. That's about half a mile from here."

"Part of this case?" I asked.

"We think so, but I can't confirm that until I get there."

"How do you know this is connected?" I watched Walker edge away from reporters.

"I think we got a phone call. But they want me to hold off on any interviews until we process the car."

His comment set off a number of cell phone conversations. I pulled mine from my hip pocket and punched the numbers to the newsroom.

"Hey Mike, this thing is starting to spread out in different directions. They think they found her car. Do you have another photographer to cover us here, until we check out the other crime scene?"

"Not a chance. Not until later in the morning. Sports is using a photog for a morning shoot."

"Okay, we'll head over there."

"Before you go Matt, the noon producer says you are now the lead. So expect the live truck."

I motioned to Ike to pack up and we joined a caravan of news units headed to the other location. We rode in silence. I glanced at my watch. There were a few hours before any news deadlines approached. A uniform blocked the street to the public but let the news cars inside the perimeter. A beige Toyota looked like it was caught in a spider web of yellow crime tape. The car tipped down to one side. The tape was lined all the way along the front of a peach stucco house. More tape stretched from a light pole to a fire hydrant.

"Flat tire," Ike said. "Look at the rear." He started pulling the camera from the back of the news van.

The Toyota rested at the edge of the street, doors closed and blocking the sidewalk. Two officers stood next to the trunk. Ike pressed against the tape, stopped, then jammed the right side of his face against the eyepiece of the camera. "Can't tell until they open the door," he whispered. "But, I think the purse is in the front seat. At least, it sure looks like a purse."

"I can't see the tag," I said, moving a few steps to my right, looking for a license plate number.

I left Ike and stood in front of the house next door to the car. A man, perhaps in his sixties, came around from the backyard.

"Excuse me," I yelled.

He started waving his hands at me. "Sorry, the detectives told me not to say too much. I'm the one who called police about the car."

He turned and bent down to look through his Ixora bushes. I figured I'd keep moving toward him until he told me to get off his property.

"Do you know who lives next door?" I asked.

"She just moved here a few months ago." His words were not directed at me but at the row of variegated ginger plants lining the front of his house. He suddenly stepped away from me, as if he spotted something in the varying shades of green.

"What are you looking for?"

"A cat."

He moved atop the grass in quick strides. I followed.

"You lose a cat?"

"Not mine, hers."

He turned to his left. A wisp of a tail curled around a corner of the hedge and disappeared.

He shouted a name which forced me to stop. I couldn't move, as if caught with stinging blows to the stomach. The last of the cool morning freshness was wearing off and I was beginning to feel hot. But not from the arcing sun. It was because of the single word.

"What did you say?"

The man turned to me, his eyebrows converged in obvious disgust with the question. "The cat! I'm trying to catch her cat." He paused, then softened his tone. "She called him Skids."

Chapter Four

My head dipped for only a moment, enough time to corner my emotions. I heard the soft impression of feet on grass. Ike moved behind me, extending a microphone toward me.

"Matt, you okay?"

"I talked to her Ike."

His face contorted into broken brow lines.

"I'm not kidding Ike! I spoke to this woman yesterday, just before my six P.M. spot. I'm positive."

"Did she give you a name?"

"No. But I heard her talking to her cat. The same one that he's holding."

The homeowner stood a few feet from us, stroking the raised fur, hugging the cat like precious cargo.

"When she gets out," the man said, "for some reason she likes my yard. My neighbor's been by here three or four times to pick her up."

He wore two sweaters on a day meant for one. Each time his wrinkled hand wove through the slate-gray fur, the cat blinked. The man's hair was two brush strokes darker than the fur he stroked. I checked my watch and raised the microphone to his chin.

"I'm Matt Bowens, Channel 14. If it's okay with you, what can you tell me about your neighbor?"

Three or four seconds passed before he answered.

"I didn't know that much about her. I know she hasn't lived here that long. I first met her when her cat wandered off."

"You see anything, or hear anything last night?"

"They told me not to say anything about that yet. But all I know is someone came by a couple of days ago, and there seemed to be some yelling at the door."

"You see who it was?"

"No . . ."

"Was the voice male or female?"

"Well, all I know is I called police this morning. Something wasn't right."

I ignored the heavy steps behind me, until a hand reached into the bent arm of the homeowner, pulling him and the cat away from the camera.

"Bowens." There was a cop's edge in his voice. I moved with them, pushing the microphone toward my moving subject.

"Did you talk to her yesterday?" I yelled.

"Bowens!"

The homeowner held on to the cat while yielding to the strong tug.

"What's your name?" I yelled.

"Lou Smith."

Detective Warren Collins released the man's arm when they reached the front door. I gave the microphone back to Ike and walked the few paces straight into the detective's glare. Before I reached him, he looked like he was about to give me another verbal warning. But this time, I pulled *him* away from the homeowner.

"I know you're busy, but when you get a moment, there's something I've got to tell you about this case."

"Okay, Bowens, what is it?"

"I'll get in touch with you later."

As I turned from Detective Collins, my right hip started to vibrate. I reached for the message on my beeper: LIVE TRUCK-WHICH LOCATION?

Camera loaded, we left a busy street of reporters and

crime techs. I telephoned Mike to have the live truck meet us where the body was found.

Frank Walker was waiting to speak at the original crime scene. He looked over his pad while we approached. Most stations had two crews on the story.

Walker's muffled grunt to clear his throat served as a warning he was ready to say something. Three cameras focused on his biscuit-sized cheeks.

"At approximately six-thirty this morning, a woman out on her morning walk discovered the body of a female. At this time, we do not know the cause of death but we believe she's been stabbed. There are no suspects and we are canvassing the area. We're asking the public, if anyone saw anything, to please call the homicide office."

"What about the house and car?" The question came from someone on my right.

"We got a phone call from a neighbor who saw her front door left open. At this time, we are waiting on a search warrant to go through the house. We processed the car and its contents and the results are part of the investigation."

"How did you make the connection between the house and the victim?" I asked.

"When she didn't show up for work, they called her house, then they contacted police," Walker said.

"So you have an ID?"

"We have her tentative identification, but we're not going to release it at this time until we have notified next of kin. I realize you all can check court records for tax statements, or run a tag, but we are asking you all to wait before releasing a name."

Other questions came from the horseshoe arrangement of reporters. "Any motive? Robbery?"

"It does not appear robbery was the motive."

"Why do you say that?"

"Let's just say we have reason to believe nothing was taken."

Walker flinched. It was usually a sign he had reached his quota of questions. But I wasn't finished.

"Did she call police about being followed?"

Walker flinched again. Two reporters took notice of the question, by staring at me. The last few breezes of the morning picked at Walker's hair. He smoothed the layered locks into place only to have the wind make them fall back into loose strands of clutter as soon as he removed his hand.

"I'll have to check on that."

We let Walker go with that final question. Behind him, Detective Collins pressed a black wingtip into the dirt. Collins waved Walker over to him, and the two talked for a few minutes before Walker came back to the collection of reporters.

"I have one thing to add."

Ike and the others raised cameras back to their shoulders.

"This afternoon, there will be a news conference at the band shell along Riverwalk. At that time, we will have more details about this case, and there will be an announcement of a reward for the arrest and conviction for the person responsible."

Walker pushed his six-foot-three and fifty-something body away from the semicircle of note takers. The live truck turned onto Franklin Avenue. Ike waved the driver to a spot near the crime tape. His truck was followed by the van from the medical examiner. Two men in white shirts and funeral-black slacks stepped out of the van, and stopped until a detective waved them forward.

I asked Walker a question away from the other reporters. "I need a hint on what will come out of the news conference."

Walker gazed at the crime scene as if to find the right words. "Since we can't confirm a name just yet, you've got to hold on to this information until later."

"I understand."

"This victim"—Walker phrased his words slow, as if picking them out of the air—"was involved in an anti-counterfeiting organization. Some high level stuff. We don't know if there's any connection, but you'll hear more details this afternoon."

"But if she—"

"That's it. Make sure you're at the news conference."

Across the field, uniforms stepped on the yellow tape until it touched the ground and the body removers walked the short distance to the side of the tarp. The hard tap on my shoulder pulled my attention from their work.

"Okay, Bowens!" Detective Collins began. "Whatcha got?"

Chapter Five

I cocked my head in the direction of the live truck and walked Detective Collins away from the ears of my colleagues.

"I got a phone call yesterday just before I went on the air. I can't be certain, but my caller had to be your victim."

The detective's eyes never showed any reaction. I guess he offered the same calm expression listening to confessions from killers and rapists. The information mattered, but his feelings stayed behind the badge.

"How can you be so sure?"

"I admit our conversation was brief, but she mentioned the name of her cat, Skids. The next door neighbor has the cat."

His jaw lowered just enough to stretch the creases which lined both sides of his face. "Thanks. We can check phone records."

He started moving away from me so I stepped off long steps toward him until I matched his walk. "Just two other things. The neighbor said someone was there, arguing with her two days ago. And if your Jane Doe is my caller, did she file reports with the police about someone stalking her? Anything on that?"

"Get back to me this afternoon." The question didn't break his stride. "I'm headed to the house and we've got an autopsy to go over this afternoon. I know you've got my beeper. But give me some time to call you back."

It wasn't much, but I had to be patient.

A thick red blanket covered her. The body removers tried to maneuver the gurney around baseball-sized rocks, and the debris in the field. The gurney wheels churned up dust and squeaked until the rollers reached the flat surface of the sidewalk. The cameras recorded the movement to the van. Before the doors were slammed shut, a uniform ripped down the yellow crime tape.

James Clemon, the live truck engineer, raised the forty-five-foot-tall television microwave mast. He configured the signal back to Miami and tugged two heavy cables from a storage rack. Clemon dragged his right hand across a moist forehead, leaving his fingers glistening with sweat.

I sat in the live truck, surrounded by television monitors, and started the process of turning raw videotape into a recognizable news story. The writing and editing took just twenty minutes. Plenty of time to go over my thoughts and prepare for a noon audience.

Just seconds after twelve, television reporters stood beneath the queen palm trees lining the street. We stared into the cameras and pointed to the spot where she was found hours earlier. My news story included the interview with Walker, and the next door neighbor. But I kept thinking about the news conference to come.

Chapter Six

A pinstriped suit appeared before the bank of microphones. Behind him, Frank Walker folded both arms into a tight knot. Television crews and newspaper reporters waited for the man in the suit to speak.

We gathered inside the gazebo next to the New River, which curved like a lifeline down the palm of Fort Lauderdale. On given Sundays, jazz bands soothed the crowds which sipped morning wine. The Florida Marlins celebrated a World Series victory here. But today, we came to gather the details of a woman dumped in a field.

"We thank you for coming," he said. "I'm William Jackels." He looked beyond the cameras, as if searching for a face, then continued to speak. "We are all saddened to hear about the death of Lane Redmond. She was a hard worker who most typified the kind of person we have asked to take on this very special job. This is a tragic loss." Jackels looked down at the podium for a few seconds, then back at Frank Walker. "You see, Lane was working on a project which could have a tremendous impact on south Florida. She was a staff member of the Hemispheric Summit on Currency."

I turned to see every reporter speeding through pages of notes. As far I could remember, no one had reported on anything called the summit on currency.

"As executive director of the committee, I knew Lane as important part of a team trying to decide where the summit

will be held next year. This will be an international conference on counterfeit money and how it can be stopped. Until
now, most of our work has been in secret. We have been qui-
etly trying to pick a site. Atlanta, New York, LA and here in
Fort Lauderdale are all being considered. Police departments and eleven nations will participate in this event,
which . . ."—his voice became lower—"will be chaired by
the president of the United States."

Jackels pulled on the beveled edges around the podium.

"Lane was working on this project when she was killed.
At this time, we do not know why she was . . . Lane was
involved in this project because she felt as we do, that the
threat of counterfeit money is on the rise. Not only from
abroad, but right here in this country. Why anyone would
harm her . . ."

He edged back two steps. Frank Walker stepped before
the microphone.

"At this time, we really can't get into too many details
about this investigation." Walker began with the same post-
death speech he had given on other murder cases. Long on
talk and stingy on facts.

"What I can tell you is that she left her home sometime
around ten P.M. Her car had a flat tire and we have reason to
believe someone might have picked her up. We still do not
have a cause of death since the autopsy is being done sometime this afternoon."

I waited for my chance to ask a question, but a thought
kept bothering me. *Why would Redmond, with access to
police, the FBI and Secret Service, call me? Was she afraid
of confiding in someone on this summit committee?*

"Frank," I said, taking a step forward, "was she on her
way to meet someone? Did the summit committee have an
emergency meeting? Was there a reason for her to leave her
house?"

Walker leaned back and stepped away from the microphones. Jackels approached.

"I can tell you that in the past we have worked some late
hours, but we did not have a meeting set for that night."

I thought about the short phone conversation and the hint that she might be a stalking victim. "Did she ever say anything to you about being followed?" I asked.

"No."

Another reporter shouted a question at the same time. One about her family.

"Her father has been contacted," Jackels said.

I joined three other reporters in a clatter of questions, but I must have shouted louder than the others. "Was there a threat of any type to members of the committee?"

They were only questions, but Jackels pushed away from the microphones without answering them. "That's all I'm going to be able to say today." His voice faded as he stepped from the podium, then he stopped. His eyes brightened and Jackels returned to microphones.

"I have just one last thing. We're in mourning because of what happened. So if you call, I may not be available. But if you have any other questions about the work of the committee, you might want to address them to someone who worked very closely with Lane. I want to introduce you to her now. She will hand out press releases about the summit."

A slender figure approached from the back with a businesslike gait. For a moment she shaded her eyes from the sun. I knew the walk. And the face. Guilt washed over me like a Florida rainstorm. I was guilty of staring at the muscled legs. If Cat ever knew I was picking up on the features and firm body lines of another woman, it would be over. The thick branches of a bulky oak tree cast a dark image on the sidewalk. She stepped through the wind-blown array of sun circles and tree shadows. Hips. Eyes. Angular face. All smooth motion, and purpose.

My head turned to watch her every step. I wasn't alone. Her hair was down, no longer pulled back behind her head. A slight breeze rolled across the bay water so her strands of hair were never able to rest at the top of her shoulders. She looked remarkably different than the night I drove her to a Fort Lauderdale hotel. If Cat was here, she could lead me away to be sentenced for staring. I'd have to plead for mercy, plant both knees on the ground and beg Cat to let my fate be swift. And Jackels could dole out the punishment. He paused until she reached the top step.

"Everyone . . . this is Stacy Gaines."

Chapter Seven

I waited until the throng packed up their cameras and tucked away writing pads. Stacy Gaines passed out sheets of information on the committee's work. A line of reporters waited for the stuff. Sandra Capers, a reporter for Channel 8, grabbed two releases. Wayne Poplin, stood off to one side. His jaw was in constant motion and the sweet jolt of peppermint gum permeated the space around him. Once part of a large public relations firm, Poplin was trying to jump-start his own company. I had interviewed him perhaps five times in the past year on projects pushed by the PR firm. Monica Sorgan from Channel 3 fidgeted in front of me. Two years out of college, Sorgan still appeared nervous in front of the camera.

I wanted to talk to Stacy without the ravenous pack listening. Her cell phone began ringing. I waited.

"Sorry." She held up an index finger and turned her phone conversation away from me.

"Your questions really intrigued them." The voice belonged to Poplin. Each time he spoke, he exposed a gray mass of gum jammed against his teeth.

"What's up, Wayne?"

"Not much. Stacy called me, so I stopped by." An excess of saliva distorted every other word.

"If this summit is awarded to . . . Fort Lauderdale, my company stands to gain. There's . . . a lot of work and a ton of money ready to be passed out." He paused and swallowed. "I'm hoping Stacy can tell if I'll get the public relations gig for the summit."

A tap on the shoulder made me turn around. Stacy motioned to Poplin to wait. I followed her down the steps of the gazebo to the street. The afternoon sun filtered through the wooden roof slats, leaving a crisscross pattern of shade on the sidewalk.

"So this is the job you couldn't tell me about?"

Stacy flashed the smile of a spin artist, her face dappled in sun darts. "I'm sorry Matt, but we were under orders. You know Jackels was waiting in the lobby when you dropped me off? He wasn't pleased to see me with a reporter."

"So what did you tell him?"

"I told him I gave away every secret we had." She coughed a soft laugh. "I told him you got nothing."

"I'll vouch for that. But what can you tell me about Lane?"

"I can't say that much. They don't want us talking."

Her eyebrows bounced up and down, against pecan skin. I ignored her warning.

"Let's start with . . . where she could have been going that night. When I dropped you off at the hotel, did she leave you a message? You two were good friends. Maybe she was coming to see you?"

"Very good friends, but I wasn't expecting her." Stacy's stare drifted to the brackish bay water as if researching my question. "I don't know where she was headed." Stacy took the remaining leaflets and slid them into a section of her briefcase.

"I just know that Lane was special. She would do any favor for me. I just had to ask. And now . . ." Stacy spoke toward the ground, but her words were directed at me. "Did the police say anything about Lane's husband?"

"Stacy . . . until now, they wouldn't give us her name. What's the deal with her husband?"

"Maybe I shouldn't say." Stacy closed up the briefcase and turned in the direction of the dark water of the New

River. Over her shoulder, incoming waves sparkled with silver lines on the surface.

"Maybe she would *want* you to say something," I said. "She reached out to me, but now, who will reach out for her? How is her husband involved in all of this?"

"I don't know if he is . . . I just know they had some pretty tough times. She had a—" Stacy pushed her hands against her forehead. When she pulled her hands away, her look changed. The eyes appeared angry. "Look, you're Cat's close friend. Because of that . . . don't overstep your welcome. You got that?"

"Whenever you want me to stand down, just say so. But we've got a killer out there with no real motive, as far as I can tell. If we stay on this story, maybe someone will pick up the phone and call homicide."

I turned in the direction of the van. But her words made me stop.

"She had a restraining order," Stacy whispered.

"Where was it issued?"

"Atlanta, I believe. We were both living there when we got the word to come south."

"Have you seen him here?"

"Jerry? No, but I've only been in the city a few weeks."

"Does he have the same last name?"

"Yes. Jerry Redmond. A real jerk." Stacy's eyes rolled.

"Do the cops know about him?"

"I have no idea."

"Why didn't you tell me about the committee?"

Her shoulders sagged. "It's a long story."

I waited, letting the silence between us bear on Stacy, forcing her to say something else. "We've been under orders, okay! Nothing to the media."

"Stacy, how long could the committee keep the work quiet, especially when we're talking about spending taxpayer dollars to pay for this?"

"It's all in that information sheet I gave you. We were about to go public in just a matter of days, but Lane's death . . ." The intensity dropped out of her voice.

"Can you put in a word for me to interview Jackels?"

Stacy gripped the briefcase and started back up the stairs where Wayne Poplin was starting to pace. He shoved his hands into his pockets.

"I'll give you this." Stacy watched the reporters getting into vans. Sandra Capers looked back at us twice then started walking in our direction.

"When her father gets here . . ." Stacy bellowed, shaking her head. "He didn't like Lane's husband and when they get her father talking, they'll never get him to shut up."

"And her father is . . . ?"

Capers stepped faster.

"Former US Senator John Priscomb."

"Didn't he make a run at the presidency?"

"It was a couple of years ago, but yes. Let's just say he didn't want to drop out of the race."

"What happened?"

"I think he should answer that."

"Doesn't he live in Tallahassee?"

"Good-bye Matt."

Capers stepped between us and aimed a question at Stacy. "Anything new?"

"Not yet."

Stacy pushed past Capers, keeping her head down until she met Poplin at the top of the stairs.

The flowers stood out because they didn't fit the picture. A dozen flamingo-pink roses were left on a rock, just a few feet from where Lane Redmond's body was found. Ike stood over the arrangement of flowers. His camera lens moved in silence, zooming into the petals.

"Any message?" I asked.

"Zip."

I wanted to look for any witnesses released by the detectives. I studied the empty lot. The tracks of the gurney from the body removal crew marked a trail in the dirt which stopped at an irregular pattern of dried blood. The roses were just off to the left. Ike raised the camera lens up from the ground.

"The person who left her here . . ." I kicked at the dirt. "There was no attempt to hide her. She was left right out in the open, as if to make a statement about something."

"Makes the whole place seem vulnerable," Ike said, squinting before shifting the camera on his shoulder and looking into the eyepiece.

I glanced left and a woman's stare connected with mine. Behind her, a row of town homes were a short walk from the lot. I stepped off the distance between us, but I didn't want to scare her.

"Afternoon," I began, still several yards away. "You live here long?"

She had a slight slouch. Her hands drifted from around her back and locked together in front of her. "Oh, about five years. Did they find the person who killed her?"

I could just make out the words. "They've only just started, but no."

"It's a shame. I saw them take her away."

A straw gardener's hat protected most of her face from the sun. The shade stopped just below her nose, exposing pale lips to the glare. In the shadow of the sweat-stained brim, wrinkle lines started at her temples and curved down along her cheeks and neck. If I could read the history of her moist eyes, it probably included a lifetime of raising children, successes and disappointments. And a grizzly-bear determination to fight the process of aging.

"Did you see or hear anything last night?"

A smile inched across her face, pulling the wrinkles tight across her cheeks. "Like I told the police, I sleep so hard, nothing could wake me up."

It was my turn to smile. "Did you see who left the flowers here?"

"I'll talk to you but not on that camera!" She pointed a bony bent finger at Ike.

"We can keep it off-camera. But you *did* see someone, right?"

She pressed her fingers into her left hand covering the gleam from her ring.

"How long have you been married?," I asked.

"Fifty-three years." She announced each word. The smile withered into a trembling lip. "But I lost him seven months ago."

"I'm sorry."

"He always said I made him laugh."

A tear started to form at the corner of her eye until she blinked a few times. The tear drop moved slowly at first, down the slope of the cheek until it disappeared inside a wrinkle.

"The man arrived in a taxicab. It was after everyone was gone. He put the roses down over there . . . waited several minutes, then got back into the cab and left."

"What did he look like?"

"Tall. Dark hair. Couldn't see his face too much."

"Younger? Older?"

"Younger. But not too young."

I thanked her. Ike waited for some signal to do an interview, but I waved him off. We loaded up the equipment, and drove to the bureau. I needed my Rolodex, and a phone call to someone who owed me a favor.

Chapter Eight

Six palm trees lined the outside of the Broward bureau like so many guards. The building faced the street but the backside opened to the bay. A four-foot-long snook kept vigil in the water but turned away as we entered through the back door. Mike Brendon's voice thundered throughout the small structure and down the hallway. "We need Sky-Fourteen over this . . . now!"

On one side of the room, three police scanners were locked on conversations about an accident. "Hazmat two, you are advised there is fuel on the highway . . ." On another channel, a male voice. Each word was laced with adrenaline. "We've got three trapped in one car, one inside the tanker, and two more in a van . . . calling for a third unit with the jaws of life." Another voice, this time the even calmness of a dispatcher. "The town of Davie, along with Fort Lauderdale Metro Fire are responding as a second alarm."

Brendon grabbed the phone and shouted. "Where's Sky-Fourteen? What do you mean they're refueling? We've got to get the helicopter over this now!" Brendon looked up at the line of televisions. Each one was set to a different television station, but so far, no one had broken into programming with the crash.

Brendon jammed the phone back to his mouth. "We've got three crews on this. I've got Dave at the hospital, waiting for ambulances, and Ron Lankin is heading to the scene.

But we need that live picture from above." Brendon looked over at me.

"Do you need us?" I asked.

Brendon shook his head. The next voice from the scanner belonged to a paramedic.

"We've got two going to BRH. Vitals on one . . . one hundred and ten over ninety . . . female with multiple contusions and a laceration to the face. We also have a four-year-old male . . . looks to be in stable condition."

Broward Regional Hospital would be ten minutes from the wreck site. Brendon kept the phone wedged against his ear. He snatched the two-way radio microphone off the desk, and pressed the mic close to his mouth. He stood there with wires and cables dangling through the thickness of his beard.

"Broward base to unit four?"

"Unit four . . ."

"Dave, you've got two coming your way, by ground."

Mike shouted into the phone. "Sky-Fourteen is in the air? Great . . . and what about a live cut-in? . . . Good." Brendon propped the phone receiver back into it's cradle and pushed the transmit button on the radio. "Unit five . . . live truck. James, how are you doing with that signal?"

"I'm raising the mast right now. I can get a signal from the camera mounted on the truck, but the crew must be two blocks from me."

"Unit eight . . . Lankin? Are you on the radio?" There was a pause before Brendon hit the button again. His voice again increased in volume. "Unit eight . . . unit eight. Ron Lankin . . . are you on the radio?"

No response.

I dialed the number to the fire department and got someone in media relations. They confirmed what we heard on the scanner. Brendon put down the microphone long enough to stroke his beard. He leveled his eyes at me through glasses, round as silver dollars.

"What do you want me to do?" I said.

"You're it Matt. Ike, get your camera. We've got a live

cut-in, special report, in four minutes. I'll brief you on what happened, and you can anchor the thing right here. You can throw to Sky-Fourteen first, then you've got a live camera on the ground from unit five . . . that's James. Ron Lankin would be doing this, but I don't where he is, and I can't reach him."

I looked around to see Ike coming in with his camera and tripod. I pushed my earpiece in place and went over in my mind what I was about to say. There was a large television monitor behind Ike. Mike recounted the series of events, until a producer's voice in my earpiece interrupted him.

"Hello Matt. We go in a few minutes. The lineup is you . . . then you go to Sky-Fourteen . . . then unit five on the ground. Is that correct?"

"That's it."

Ike flipped a switch and I immediately felt the heat from three studio lights. I waited for the jingle music and graphic saying this was a break from regular programming. I had my basic facts, but I would have to use the monitor as my script. I waited until I saw myself on television before I spoke.

"Good afternoon, I'm Matt Bowens and this is a special report from the Fort Lauderdale newsroom. We've got a massive tie-up on northbound interstate ninety-five near Broward Boulevard. From Sky-Fourteen, you can see a tanker truck has flipped over on it's side. A haz-mat . . . or hazardous materials unit is there . . ."

The camera from the helicopter zoomed in on the tanker. I heard the producer in my ear.

"You're hot, Sky-Fourteen."

I focused on the moving pictures. "From what we under-stand from the fire department, the driver in one car was cut off by the tanker truck and caused the truck to turn over. A van behind the truck was also involved. We have another angle from down on the ground . . ." As I spoke, Miami punched up the camera mounted on the top of the live truck. The picture changed to an angle at street level.

"There are fire units from three different departments. We understand firefighters used the jaws of life to remove two people from the van. They are being rushed to Broward

Regional Hospital. There is no word on the driver of the truck. A portion of the interstate has been shut down, and traffic is backed up all the way to Sheridan Street."

I talked for another thirty seconds before throwing it back to regular programming. I pulled out my earpiece and stepped away from the lights. Brendon was on the phone, talking to someone about Greenbound Trucking. It was the name on the side of the truck cab. I waited to see if he still needed me. Brendon pushed the phone away from his mouth.

"Thanks," he said. "Stay on the murder. Lankin will pick up the tanker for the afternoon."

Any thoughts on getting lunch were a distant memory. I'll make it up at dinner, I reasoned. My Rolodex contained the names of dozens of contacts and police agencies. There was also a card for Southtown Cabs. They handled most of Fort Lauderdale and I knew the day shift dispatcher. I dialed the number.

"Hello, is Rollo there?"

"Rollo? What a minute." The man's voice on the phone was rich with a Jamaican accent. "He has a break in . . . five minutes. You call back?"

"No problem. Oh, and tell him Matt called."

I put the phone down and grabbed two videotapes of the murder scene, ready to go over the pictures. The phone rang again, so I eased back into the chair.

"Matt, what is it and hurry? Got two cabs with flat tires, and another at the airport who wants to call a general strike over wages."

"Hello Rollo, getting ready for early retirement again?"

"You've got thirty seconds Matt, I got to get back."

"Someone picked up a fare this afternoon and went to Ranklin Avenue . . . the spot where they found a body this morning. He waited a few minutes and left. I need to know where he was dropped off."

"Hold a sec."

I could hear a mixture of voices and engines being revved. The voice belonged to Rollo, but I could only make out a few of the words.

"Matt, you still there?"

"Are you kidding, and miss the exciting world of driving a cab?"

"All right Matt . . . and how badly do you need the information?"

"Okay . . . okay . . . you've got my attention."

"Let me run this by the boss," he said.

I waited several minutes and I was about to hang up when Rollo came back on the line.

"Here's the deal. You caught him on a good day. The boss wants to be up front about this. If anyone calls, we'll give out the information. But so far, you're the only who figured out we picked up the fare."

"So, what do you have?"

"The fare was dropped off at the Clouden Inn, the one over on Dixie Highway in Oakland Park."

"What about a name? Did the driver say if he was nervous or upset?"

"Next you'll be asking if we take a pulse and do background checks! How do I know? Driver says the man didn't talk."

"Thanks Rollo." Someone in the background was screaming.

I checked my watch. Two and a half hours until news time. I had to get started on a script, but I wanted to get in a few more phone calls. Two rings and I got an answer.

"Clouden Inn . . . Oakland Park. May I help you?"

The man sounded like he had repeated the line so many times, it bored him to say the name.

"Yes, I'm looking for . . ."

"Yes sir?" A voice yawned through the words.

I waited until I thought I had his attention. "I'm trying to reach a Jerry Redmond."

"Hold on, let me check." A melodic flow of classical music took over for the impatient desk clerk.

"Hello sir, I'm showing he checked out this afternoon."

"How long ago?"

"Hmm . . . in fact, I checked him out just minutes ago."

"Do you see him in the lobby?"

"No."

"Well, can you take a look? I have to reach him."

"Sir, if you will just hold on. I do have guests waiting in line here."

"Listen, thank you for your help. But please, just take a look and see if he's still there."

No music this time, just the loud clang of the phone being dropped on the counter. Behind me, Ike walked the pace of a photographer on deadline.

"Hello. I made a mistake. Someone else checked out. Mr. Redmond is still here."

"Can you connect me?"

"One moment please."

The ring had a hollow sound from the hotel's internal system.

"Hello."

"Mr. Redmond?"

"Yes."

"This is Matt Bowens, with Channel Fourteen news. I'm sorry to hear about Lane."

There was a long pause before he answered. "I don't know what to say. I'm still in shock."

"Is it okay if I speak to you? It won't take—"

"I'm not sure about that."

"I'm interested in the things you remember about Lane."

Another pause. "Like I said, I'm not sure."

"I'll tell you what. Let me head your way and if you don't want to say anything, that's up to you. What room are you in?"

"Three-oh-eight."

"Thank you." I lowered the phone and turned toward the assignment desk. "Mike, I want to work tonight."

Mike Brendon aimed a finger at his glasses and pushed them back into position. "If there's a follow-up, let the night team do it."

"I want to do this. I found the husband."

Mike's smile revealed a white line of teeth through the

whiskers. "Okay. Ike . . . you up for some overtime to work with him?"

"Sure, he'll work," I said. "Look at all that money he'll rack up."

"Where is he?" Mike adjusted his body to get a fresh squat in his chair.

"The Clouden Inn. I figure we'll rush over there after my hit at five o'clock."

"You're taking a chance he'll still be there."

"Don't have a choice Mike, I've got the newscast to worry about first."

The next twenty minutes were a blur of forming a script, pulling videotape, and speaking my written words into a microphone to be recorded. I left Ike in the booth, so he could edit the final package. Ike matched my words and his video. I had more phone calls to make. After getting a number from directory assistance, I dialed Tallahassee.

"Hello, is Mr. Priscomb there?"

"No," a female voice answered. The one word was full of emotion, as if she had been crying.

"Is Mr. Priscomb—"

"We can't say anything right now, except Mr. Priscomb is getting ready to drive to Fort Lauderdale." The even peal of dial tone ended the conversation.

I dialed the police department. The lead detective wasn't in, so I settled for the public information officer. Walker gave me the standard answer that there was nothing new in the investigation.

Ike emerged from the edit booth fifteen minutes later and we sent our edited story to Miami by microwave. Then we drove to the house on Ninth, so I could stand in front of a live camera and tell south Florida everything I knew about Lane Redmond. After my live words, a director in Miami would hit a button and play the edited package.

Still, Jerry Redmond bothered me. If pressed, I could explain his actions, but I wanted to ask him about the restraining order and why he was leaving town after his wife was found murdered?

Chapter Nine

Once inside the Clouden Inn, I almost bumped into a woman standing next to a large suitcase. I didn't see anyone who fit Redmond's description.

I walked back outside through the huge double doors and motioned to Ike. We entered the lobby and headed for the elevators off to the left. If someone from security stopped us, we would have to leave or convince them we were invited upstairs.

The elevator opened to the third floor and quiet replaced the din from the lobby. Several seconds passed as we looked down the hallway through the dim light. A door opened, and fluorescent light illuminated a section of the hallway and the suitcase resting in the middle of the hallway. We stepped closer. The numbers dropped in succession as the door started to close: 308. I stepped faster. The door opened again.

I recognized him even though I had never seen him before. He seemed trapped in the old Miami Vice look. A beige sport coat fitted loosely over his black silk T-shirt. The matching beige slacks had a smudge on one knee. Polished loafers, and no socks. When he moved, a plastic watch band appeared and reappeared from under the sleeve of the sport coat. The only thing missing was a thick gold chain. But I figured he pawned that to pay for the plane ticket to Fort Lauderdale. I extended my hand. "Mr. Redmond. Matt Bowens, Channel Fourteen News. I know this is a hard time for you."

"You don't have any idea how hard it is."

"Again, we really wanted to talk to you about Lane."

"How did you find me?"

"What we've been told about Lane is very limited. We're just trying to find out more about her."

It was that moment in the conversation when he could slam the door shut or invite us inside. "And I just wanted to tell you where you could find your cat." I backed up a step, giving him an ample chance to call security and tell me to get out.

"Somebody has Skids?"

"Lane's next door neighbor has him."

The squared edges in the shoulders of his sport coat sagged just a bit.

"I was the one who named him, you know. We found him in an alley off Peach Street in Atlanta. He came right up to Lane, like he knew everything would be safe with her, like everyone did."

"Do you have a picture of her?"

Redmond shoved a right hand in his pocket, and pulled out a two-inch-thick wallet. "C'mon in." He motioned us inside, then pulled his suitcase back into the room.

"You say you named him Skids?"

Redmond coaxed two pictures from the wallet and handed them to Ike. He propped them up on the dresser and set up his tripod. Now there was a face instead of the vision of a woman found in a field.

"I named him that because that's where my life was at that time . . . on the skids. That cat had more going for him than I did. Lane took me in—" His voice softened.

"Can we ask you a few questions?"

"A few. I've got to check out and catch a plane. But . . . I really shouldn't be doing this."

Ike moved on to the second picture. In the first photograph, Lane's hair was long. Longer than shoulder length. One layer of curls dipped down past her left eye. The smile was wide and she appeared happy. In the second photograph, the hair was cut short, and the grin looked forced.

"That first picture is the way I met her. She was going to the University of Florida," Redmond said, admiring the picture. "We met at a football game. She has a beautiful smile."

In the years of covering stories in south Florida, victim's families always referred to loved ones in the present tense. The sudden loss of a husband, wife, son or daughter, with no chance of saying good-bye, was too much. All thoughts about them were still locked on the present as if they were alive and about to walk through the door.

"Thank you for the picture. Again, is it okay if we just ask you a question about Lane?"

Redmond flashed me an expression I've seen on others who didn't know whether to pursue the truth or hide from it.

"What channel did you say you were from?"

"Channel Fourteen."

"I don't know if I . . ." Each word from Redmond was labored.

"You mean because of the restraining order?"

He paused. "Yes, there was an order, but I didn't go near Lane. She can tell you that . . . I mean . . ." Redmond sank in the bed nearest the window. "I never went to her. The only reason I came here was to see her at a neutral location. I want to make up and start over."

"The neighbor says he saw someone arguing with her the night before . . . they found her."

"I suppose you want me to say it was me?"

"I just want to ask you about the Lane Redmond you remember."

"Okay. Just a few questions."

Ike moved the tripod and aimed the camera toward Jerry Redmond's worried expression. I opened my pad. The light on the camera meant Ike was recording. "Lane was described as hard working. What else can you tell us about her?"

"She is the only one who believed in me." Redmond rubbed a thumb across both eyes. "She sees things in me that made me want to change . . . and now she is gone."

"Did she say anything to you about being stalked?"

"Me? No. Did someone say that? I haven't really talked to her for a while."

"Did you see her while you were here?"

"You mean, did I violate my restraining order?"

"Didn't you? Wasn't it you seen arguing with Lane?"

"No. I loved Lane. If anything, I was trying to make things right. And I didn't violate the order."

"You weren't at her house?"

"No."

"But now you're leaving?"

"I was going to call her, but I changed my mind. After I heard about what happened . . . I went . . . and left some roses. She liked the pink ones."

"Have you gone to the police?"

Redmond held up a hand. "No more. That's it. No more questions. Please leave, now."

When we didn't move right away, he repeated his demand for us to go. I signaled Ike to turn off the camera. Redmond pulled tight on the lapels of his sport coat until the T-shirt was no longer visible. "Why are you getting into that?" he said.

"I just thought that if your wife is found dead, then you'd be contacting authorities to find out what happened."

"Maybe I have."

"So you've been in touch with Detective Collins?"

Anyone who carries a reporter pad has to be able to read faces. And Redmond's unsteady eyes kept telling me deception.

"I can't remember who I talked with. Someone in homicide. Listen, I need you guys to go. We're done here, right?"

"One last question. Was Lane close to her father?"

"Senator idiot?" Redmond's face turned ashen, like the person who said the wrong words and wanted to pull the words back into his mouth. "I didn't mean that."

"It's fine. We have your other statements. I was just curious about her father."

"He wasn't my biggest fan." He paused. "Lane's father is

the reason for the restraining order. He pushed her into doing it."

"Why would he do that—"

"Because I questioned some of his dealings."

"I don't understand."

"If I could just talk to Lane, I could get all this resolved, but Mr. Senator had other ideas." He looked at his watch. "I don't want to say anymore."

I pulled out a business card and pointed it at Redmond's sneer. "We'll go. But I'd like to stay in touch. There's my number."

We backed into the hallway and watched the door close with a soft click.

By the time I reached the bureau, my pager railed against my side. I dialed up the number for the nighttime assignment editor.

"We're back in the office, what's up?"

"The police called. They're very interested in what Redmond told you. They even suggested they wanted the raw tape." Wade Summer was a fixture on nights for six years.

"Whatever we put on the air, they can have. The rest, they'll have to fight with our attorneys in court."

"Well, that's what I told them, basically. What did he say?"

I could tell Summer wanted some bombshell. Perhaps a confession. "I should have called you earlier. He says he didn't go to see Lane, but I have my doubts, big time. We also got a picture."

"Matt, the producer wants some of that video to tease your story."

"How did the police know about Redmond?"

"I think they started tracking him down by way of Atlanta and then found out he took a plane here. Frank Walker told me it all fell together when someone from the hotel called police to complain about you. That's how they found out where he was."

"You mean they dragged him from the hotel, and we're not there?" I tried to keep my voice down to an accepted office volume.

"Walker says Redmond was already in custody when he called me. But he's not under arrest. Walker wanted to make that clear. He's in for questioning and a Georgia hold for violation of the restraining order. I've got another crew waiting at the police station, just in case they release him."

"Okay. Later."

I worked on the script and kept flicking a glance up at the monitors. I pushed aside any concerns about the competition getting to the hotel. Any suspicions were realized just before news time. My story was finished and microwaved to Miami. But on Channel 8, Sandra Capers was already teasing her exclusive story. Capers was there to get video of Redmond being taken away from the hotel.

Our stories ran at about the same time. Capers had exclusive video of Redmond lowering his head, while being eased into a police unit. She had her video, but I had the exclusive interview.

"Someone tipped her." Each word from Ike sounded like defeat. I reached to lower the volume of both monitors. I kept my arm in motion, swinging from the bank of televisions until I slapped my fist against a stack of phone books.

"She still didn't get the sound!" Ike yelled, trying to calm me down. I called Rollo and was told that he didn't receive any other calls beside mine.

"The desk clerk," I said. "He must have called Capers."

Chapter Ten

"Why didn't you tell me?"

Cat let my question linger, unanswered for several seconds.

"Tell you what?" Cat poked at the sausage and green peppers. The crackle of pork-skin on a hot skillet released an aroma reminding me of vendors preparing ropes of pork and sliced green peppers on the streets of Chicago.

"Why didn't you tell me where Stacy was working?"

"Just 'cause you're a reporter, you don't have to know everything."

"Any more secrets I should know about?"

Cat tossed in another layer of peppers and ignored my question. The voice of Luther Vandross drifted from the CD player in the family room. Cat sang along with him until it was time to scold me. Finally she said, "And if I told you about Stacy's job, what would you do with the information?"

My response came several seconds later. "I would have turned that into a story."

"Exactly. A story about Stacy and the committee, after she told me she didn't want anything out yet. I know what's on your mind, Matt. That's why I didn't say anything."

I took in the aroma-filled air. Cat stared at me. "And then there's my job."

"The bank wouldn't have anything to do with this."

"I'm a bank teller, Matt. The bank doesn't want to be linked to anything being released too soon. And that means me."

"Okay." I held up my hands in surrender.

"But I don't want to be there forever." Cat spoke soft, almost to herself.

"You mean the bank?"

"I don't know how I can fit all this in. I've got my hours at the office, I take one college course in the afternoon, and then I have to be back to pick up Jason at preschool and get ready for dinner." I saw her arms moving, hands picking up ingredients. She talked over her shoulder. "That's why I'm up late, cooking tomorrow's dinner now, I'm behind on my research paper, and you're asking me about secrets?"

"At least the bank lets you shape your hours so you can do this."

Cat gave my words no response. The clock behind her was partially hidden by the dangling vines of a philoden-dron, but it was past midnight.

"So, you knew about the committee's work?"

She blinked. "Sure I knew. But she also asked me to keep it quiet." She pointed a grease-laden fingertip at me. "And that means you. I didn't want to be your tipster on the com-mittee." Cat paused. "It's just so sad about Lane. Any idea who did it?"

"Not really. They questioned the husband."

Cat sprinkled spice after spice into the frying pan. All of it became part of the sizzle. Garlic, onion powder and a few shakes from an unlabeled container.

"What's that?" I sounded like the visitor on some cook-ing show.

"It's a secret," Cat smiled proudly. "It's my own stuff." Her eyes gleamed hues of copper and gray.

"I want you to know something about me and Stacy." Her voice took on a smooth, even tone. "I met my ex in college. I fell for his lines and the big smile. I couldn't see past that smile."

Cat stroked the entire pan of sausage and peppers into a glass container lined with paper towels, and stuffed the hot mix in the fridge. "It was Stacy who told me to slow down."

I squirmed a bit in my chair, clearly uncomfortable with

hearing details about Cat's desire for another man. She must have sensed my uneasiness.

"You opened up this door," she said. "There's a lot of history between me and Stacy. If you want to hear everything . . ."

The door to the fridge was still open and Cat pushed it shut so hard the plant shook. "I should have listened to her. He turned out to be a player, a lowlife thug. The man never worked. He had an excuse for everything, and the only things he cared about were himself, a scam and the next woman."

Until now, I never raised any questions about her ex-husband. It was an area I tried to avoid. Cat stared at me. "The best thing is I've got two beautiful children. But . . . I'm raising them and their father's in prison."

Cat grabbed the spatula and started the cooking process again. She raked through another helping of sliced pepper and meat causing grease to slop over the edge of the pan near the hot burner.

"What am I doing?" Cat whispered, reaching for a towel to wipe the grease from the stove top. A trail of smoke drifted upward from the burner and Cat touched a button, turning on the hood fan.

"I'm gonna burn this house down."

"So Stacy's always been there for you?"

"She's been there for me, but I haven't always been there for her. She tried to protect me. What was the first thing she did when she got a chance to ask you some questions?"

"She grilled me."

"Exactly. I'm surprised she didn't ask you for a urine sample."

I was again caught by the scent of cooked peppers. "And Stacy was a grad student?"

"No, no, no. Undergrad. I met Stacy during registration when we were both fighting over the last seat in Professor Minor's sociology class. I really needed that class. Stacy gave up the seat for me."

She wiped her forehead. "My life was so fast then. Classes, new boyfriend. I just feel . . ."

"What's bothering you?"

"It's just I can remember all the times Stacy came through for me, and plenty of times when I wasn't there for her. Things were moving so fast, I could barely take care of myself. I always thought Stacy understood. But we never talked about it."

Cat's hazel eyes reflected a warmth. The minutes passed until the container was again removed from the fridge and the cooked sausage was added to the stack of meat.

"Wait a minute." She stepped away and into the other room.

Cat eased back into the kitchen. "How's this?" She turned off the lights and set a lit candle on the table. The flickering shadows caught her eyes.

"Matt?" Her voice broke my stupor and I glanced up at the clock. "Still thinking about secrets?" Cat smiled. The last word came out hard. Her breath caused the thin line of candle smoke to break into dozens of twisting circles. " 'Cause I really don't have any—"

I caught her in mid-sentence, pushing into her lips, while she pulled me into her, tight against her stomach. Her hands reached around my back and she locked her fingers in a gentle hug. She smelled of fresh flowers, ginger mint and spices. When she finally pulled away, Cat blew out the candle, and grabbed my hand. Whispers and darkness.

Chapter Eleven

I eased the tripod down on the black marble. Stacy Gaines had her hair pulled back and she was wearing a navy-blue dress with velvet trim. Her shadow-gray pumps blended into the floor.

"He'll see you in a few minutes." She gave me a business smile, checked over some items on a list and left us in the waiting room. The summit committee had offices on the fifth floor of the Hanson Building. Oak paneling, ceiling to floor. Nothing like the concrete cinder block walls and dank hallway smell of my Chicago housing project.

"He'll see you now." Stacy led us through a hallway topped with track lights directing bright beams on huge paintings. The marble tile ended, and the black Berber rug in Jackels' office softened our footsteps.

"Morning, Mr. Bowens." The voice came out of the suit. Behind Jackels, three shelves were lined with photographs. No family pictures, just wooden-framed pics of Jackels with past presidents, drug enforcers, and a retired NFL quarterback. Ike set up the camera gear.

"Was Lane a part of the committee from the beginning?" My question was meant as a warm-up. The camera wasn't even on.

"Where are you going with this?" Jackels played with the items on his desk, and blew the dust off a small globe, as if I came to inspect for cleanliness.

"Don't worry. Ike will shoot above the desk." I grabbed one of his business cards out of a gold-plated holder. "I just wondered if she's been here since the committee was formed?"

Stacy took up a spot on the couch behind me. "Matt's just trying to get a sort of history behind our work." It sounded like support from Stacy. Jackels let his eyes drift between her and the camera, finally resting on me. He finished rearranging his desk.

"It's just that we've been so . . . quiet about our interests up to now."

Stacy took out her pad, jotting down notes as we talked.

"Go ahead." Ike said. The camera was recording.

"Can you tell me why anyone would want to harm Lane Redmond?" I asked.

Jackels grabbed a pen and held it off to his side in the air. "Lane was the most gracious, hardworking person you could meet. She would stay here late into the night, prepping for meetings, and then beat me here in the morning. No, I can't imagine why anyone would harm her."

He jabbed the air with the pen with each sentence.

"Did she ever come to you about being followed?"

"At some point, some matters relating to this will have to be avoided since there is an ongoing investigation, but no, she never came to me about being followed or stalked."

"Do you know why she would call me the night before she was murdered?"

Jackels aimed the pen at me. "Called you? How do you know that? The police never said . . . turn the camera off for a moment." Ike kept rolling. "Turn the camera off right now!"

"Okay Ike." My whisper grew louder. "Ike." Ike tapped the button to stop the camera.

"She called me asking for information about stalking," I told him.

Stacy's hands kept scrawling notes across the page. Jackels stood up from his desk, and tossed the pen on his calendar. "The police never said anything about that."

"One, I told Detective Collins about the phone call. And two, they're not going to tip you to everything they're working on. In their eyes, everyone is a suspect. I'm just trying to fill in the blanks . . . those days and hours leading up to her death. And I really need to know why she called me instead of picking up the phone and calling you. Ike turn it back on."

The decision belonged to Jackels. Either he could sit down and talk to me or walk out of the room. I looked back at Stacy. She stopped writing. I waited to see if she would say something to Jackels.

Silence.

I turned back to Jackels and his converging eyebrows.

"How do you know it was Lane?" He eased back into his chair, glanced at Ike and the camera before waiting for an answer.

"She didn't mention her name, but I have enough to tell me it was her. Lane wouldn't call a reporter unless she was desperate to get someone's attention."

Jackels leaned forward in his chair. "I don't know why she called. If she called. Maybe she felt she couldn't talk to me. But we had a good working relationship."

"Could there be something else?"

Ike tapped the controls, probably to zoom in on the face in front of me. Jackels pulled on the lapels of his suit.

"No. I would have known. We are entrusted with some high level information, but I doubt if anyone got to her."

The brow lines in Jackels' face flattened into a single crack above his eyes. "We're getting into areas reserved for the police investigation."

"The way she was dressed when they found her," I began. "Almost as if she was called to some kind of meeting. Was she supposed to meet someone here?"

"Again, you're drifting into matters that I think should be reserved for the detectives."

"Was she meeting you?"

"Mr. Bowens, I stand on my previous statement. It's in police hands now."

"And her work here on the committee?"

"For one thing, Lane was set to get information out to the public. It was her main concern. She had a voice in the companies we hired."

"Companies?"

"Everything from firms tracking information on counterfeiting trends, to setting up regional meetings with bank investigators."

Jackels paused as if to remember more of her duties. "And she was part of a specialized group. Aside from picking a site for the conference, she tried to answer how counterfeit money was getting into the United States? How are people in this country making fake bills? Who are the major players? for instance. This is a private-slash-government organization. We are not the Secret Service, but we work closely with them and we receive some federal money. Our main function is to coordinate with the banking industry to make sure we can control counterfeiting."

"And how bad is the problem?"

Jackels took in a chest full of air as if to start a speech, then grabbed the pen again. "You can't go into a store anymore without seeing a sign saying they won't take fifties and hundreds. Mom and Pop joints won't even bother with big bills. It wasn't that way even ten years ago. We make a change, and the counterfeiters adjust. Kids think they can make bills on their laser printer. The problem is national and worldwide. Still, this conference is aimed at making a hemispheric effort to show all other countries that it's in their best interest to help stop the flow of bad dollars."

Jackels started to get up, then looked at the microphone connected to his tie and stopped. "Can I show you something?"

Ike showed him he could move with the mic. Jackels walked past the line of pictures.

"Quite impressive, isn't it?" He pointed a finger toward the corner. "That's one of my favorites." A picture showed a smiling Jackels burning a wad of money. Jackels stopped at a closet door.

"Bogus?" I asked.

"We confiscated two million that week. All fake."

I inspected the picture. The money looked real. Jackels slid open a keypad on the wall and tapped in a code. A door rolled away from view, disappearing inside a wall with a low hiss, and revealing a sealed compartment. Ike worked the controls of the camera, and aimed the lens at the door. Jackels waved us inside a room. I thought I was in lotto heaven. On a table, spread out like some jackpot winnings, were stacks of bills. A tall pile of hundreds. Fifties. The table was covered in green mounds.

"Take a look at it." Jackels smiled.

Ike aimed his camera at me as I picked up three stacks of hundred-dollar bills. They had a certain flat feel to them. I checked each stack looking for flaws. "These are pretty good. Where did you get them?"

"They were found inside the walls of car radiators, coming in from out of the country. We ripped up the car before we hit pay dirt. If we were wrong, the government was on the hook for thousands in damages. But our tip was correct."

"Your tip?"

"From time to time we get solid leads called in to us and we pass them onto the Secret Service. We know the bogus makers have all kinds of tricks, but if you take a good look at the money, you'll spot the flaws."

"And counterfeiting is catching on locally?" I asked.

"Bars are a favorite target. And we're catching teens passing them in drugstores."

"Was Lane in on the investigations?"

"No. Lane's not part of the Secret Service, and again, we're not either. However, if we catch the tip, they will keep us involved in ongoing cases."

I tossed the stacks of fake bills on the heap. Ike's lens followed the money landing on the table.

"Imagine . . . this is just one shipment. A lot of stuff is getting through or being made in small lots by amateurs." Jackels sounded like he was addressing lawmakers. He picked up a stack of pale green bills and held them close to his face.

"There is a war going on. A war over our own currency. And the bad guys know if we let our money get compromised, we lose stature, both here, and with all countries."

Ike held the shot aimed at Jackels. I glanced over the piles and posed a question. "Could Lane have been the target of some group . . . perhaps someone under investigation?"

"We have to take a look at all of the elements into Lane's death, even the possibility she was somehow tipping others about probes. She was not in a position to be directly involved in investigations, but it cannot be ruled out because she was privy to high-level information."

Stacy stood in the door waiting. "Are we through here?" Jackels flipped a stack of fifties on the pile.

"We're done."

Stacy walked us to the elevators. She turned in the direction of heels hitting the hard marble. "Pardon me." The secretary handed her a note. The elevator door opened. Ike started to board, but I made him stop.

"What's up Matt?" Ike eased the heavy equipment to the floor.

"Just wait," I told him. Stacy held the note for a moment then swept thin fingers across the top of her slate-black hair. A worried look replaced the calm face. "What's wrong?" I asked.

Stacy waved the note in the air as she talked. "That was the hotel. Something happened . . . or rather didn't happen. I don't know. I've got to get back there."

"Can I help?"

"No. I'll be all right."

"You sure?"

"Positive. Go."

Chapter Twelve

Frank Walker kept us corralled off to one side of the police station. "This is the way it's going to go," he said. "No exceptions. Jerry Redmond is being released in a few minutes. He's been here all night. This is not a perp walk. The man is free to go."

"No charges at this time?" I yelled.

"No charges. And I want to make it clear about this. We are not, repeat not, calling him a suspect. If any of you call him that, it's your lawsuit."

"Does he have an attorney?" The question came from another reporter.

"He has representation," Walker said.

"Did he answer all your questions?" I asked.

"Mr. Redmond was very cooperative, but beyond that, I can't say anything more at this time. We just don't want you to rush him once he walks out the door."

Walker surveyed the group inching toward the front door. "Stand back, or we'll have to move all of you across the street." Walker held up his hands, trying to be traffic cop to four television cameras and two still photographers. Rank and file uniforms called the building the pillbox.

We had left Jackels' office and Mike Brendon directed us to the police station. We arrived last. Ike kicked away a beer can to make way for his tripod. My pager vibrated a steady throb against my hip. I checked the message.

"They want us in the noon show," I told Ike.

We waited five minutes. Ten minutes became twenty. Walker promised us a warning before Redmond came out. He lied. Jerry Redmond stepped through the front doors and dropped his head as soon as the sunlight touched him. Photographers jumped to their cameras, and took aim, like runners getting up to the start line.

Redmond looked dead pale. A huge stain covered the front of his jacket and shirt. Reporters shouted questions but the zombie didn't reply. A large figure followed Redmond and strolled from the pillbox, then picked up his pace until his steps matched Redmond's slow gait. We never saw Tank Robinson on just *any* case. Only the big ones. The attorney's six-foot-four height, bald head, and bison girth earned him the nickname. Tank grabbed Redmond's arm, guiding him to a red Porsche. The smell of Redmond's clothing reached us before he could get close. The putrid aroma of dried vomit drifted over us. Ike winced.

Robinson eased Redmond into the passenger seat and marched toward the cameras. He stopped and waited until every lens was focused on his bullet-contoured frame.

"Mr. Redmond is very distraught. He has been through a terrible night. The horrid details and crime scene photographs placed before Mr. Redmond sickened him. With any heinous death, family members are always suspect. We understand that. He answered all their questions because we want the person or persons responsible for this horrible murder to be brought to justice."

I launched a question, knowing police probably went over the same ground with Redmond. "I understand there is a restraining order against him. Did he try to see Lane before her death?"

"Mr. Redmond saw his wife briefly, but that was it. He left and went to his hotel room."

I shouted a follow-up. "He told me he didn't see her."

Tank smiled at me. "Like I said, he saw Lane for just a few moments at her home and went to the hotel."

"He was there the entire night?"

"He stayed in his room until he saw the news. Mr. Redmond had to find out about his wife's death by seeing her house on television. He got into a cab and left flowers at the crime scene. I'm sorry but I have to move on."

"Why didn't he go straight to the police?" I shouted.

Tank ignored me. He pushed a meaty palm into his suit and withdrew a handful of business cards. He was doling them out like the best dealer in Vegas. And then he was gone. The Porsche hummed through the parking lot until the engine revved to a high-pitched strain into the morning traffic.

I looked at my watch: 11:10. The live truck rolled into the parking lot. Less than an hour later, I faced a camera and spewed the facts gathered in the morning. I used the video shot by Ike: Jerry Redmond leaving the police station, the interview with Tank, and a short portion of the comments from Jackels. After my one-minute-thirty contribution to the noon show, we eased into the office, loaded down with fast-food burgers.

A tall partially gray-haired man stood in the middle of the small newsroom. Mike Brendon was off to one side and appeared nervous. The man extended his hand. His grip squeezed the blood in my fingers back up into my arm.

"Mr. Bowens . . . I'm John Priscomb. I'm Lane's father."

Chapter Thirteen

"What do you know about my daughter's death?" His voice offered no emotion, not even at the mention of his daughter. But he couldn't hide the roiling anger in his eyes.

"I only spoke to her briefly on the phone. She wanted to talk to me about stalkers."

"Stalkers?" Grief seeped into his eyes, as if he tried to consider the danger Lane faced before her death. "This is the first I'm hearing about stalking. She give any hint as to who might be following her?"

"No. I'm sorry I can't give you more details. I could sense in her voice there was a lot more to what she was telling me."

The former senator aimed a thumb at the bank of televisions behind him. "I saw my son-in-law on all the stations . . . see he's got a lawyer already. After I leave here, I'm going to see him next."

"You have concerns about him?" I braced for the political answer, full of well-rounded words, and short on meaning or impact.

"I plan to express my concerns to the police," he said.

"Mr. Redmond says you tried to break up the marriage."

"He would say that. This coming from a man who hasn't had a steady job in three years. Did you ask him why he's here?"

"I did."

"And?"

"He says he wanted to patch things up with your daughter."

"I'll bet. They need to find out where he was."

Priscomb's fingers curled tight into a fist.

"Mr. Priscomb . . . any reason why your daughter would call me instead—"

"My wife is out in the car. She can barely move. We only had one child. You can't imagine what my wife is going through. We sent our daughter down here to be a part of something we thought was important. Now we're going to bury her."

The words flowed. Crisp. Composed. His hair was a layered mixture of black lines and worn silver, like stacks of dirty coins. The chin was firm and tanned and his eyes never broke their concentration on my face. The shoes reflected a bright shine. He wore a navy and gray tie, and his suit was just the right shade of politician-blue.

"Is it okay if we speak to you on camera?"

He paused. "Not right now. I'm sure you'll understand and respect what we're going through. What we're trying to do now is gather facts, as painful as they might be, and try to get a read on what happened. At some point, soon, very soon, I will sit down with you. I promise. Lane was the kind of person I'm proud to speak about."

"Did she call you in the past few weeks?"

"We talked, but she didn't say anything was bothering her." Priscomb eased the door open wide enough to reveal a white Lexus at the curb. He turned back to me. "I have just one other question. Did my daughter mention a name? Someone giving her problems at work?"

"A name? No. We didn't get that far."

As Priscomb got into the car, a woman sat in the passenger seat, dabbing at her eyes. Her cheeks glistened under the interior lights. A family always groomed and poised for public decorum now had to deal with the death of a daughter. Again, Priscomb's eyes locked steady with mine as if he wanted to shake the building from it's foundations and see what facts fell to the ground. Perhaps at one time he had the power to rattle underlings, and make lobbyists tremble. Now he just looked like a father looking for answers.

"There's a message for you." Mike Brendon pointed to a pink square of paper in my mailbox. "Somebody named Stacy called. The number's there."

I grabbed the message and dialed. A woman answered.

"Hotel Camdon."

"I'm trying to reach the room of Stacy Gaines."

"Are you Mr. Bowens?"

"Yes."

"She's been waiting for your call. Just a minute."

I listened to the soft clang of phone equipment landing on something solid. Unintelligible voices. Desk clerks helping hotel guests.

"Matt?"

"Stacy, what's wrong?"

"Someone tried to get into my hotel room. I called Jackels. The police are here."

"Is there anything of value in your room?"

"Just a few files. Nothing important."

"Did they break the lock?"

"I have a key card. But police say they probably tried to jam something into the slot but it didn't open."

"Any witnesses?"

"No. They probably got frustrated and left. But the door is all scratched up. The maid noticed it."

"What about surveillance cameras in the hallway?"

"Like a lot of hotels, I don't think they have them. Matt, I don't like this. I've got a rental car. I've got to get away from here for one night. I've been trying to get in touch with Cat. Can you let her know I'm staying at her house tonight?"

"No problem. Will you be okay until I get there later?"

"Sure . . . I don't want any coverage on this. Don't bring any cameras. Let's not make this into something, when it could be very minor."

Chapter Fourteen

"**I** need your help." My question resulted in a look of concern from Wayne Poplin. I stood in a small two-bedroom house, converted into an office. Southeast Tenth Street included more than a dozen Fort Lauderdale homes, all retrofitted into office space. I leaned on the brick fireplace.

"You sure you need *my* help?" Poplin chewed on his usual concoction of several sticks of gum. A huge sign covered a section of the wall: WAYNE POPLIN—PUBLIC RELATIONS. I decided to approach Poplin because of his knowledge of everyone in south Florida.

"I need more information on the committee's work," I started. "Where did the committee members come from? Background information not provided in their press release."

Poplin pulled his attention from a computer. Ike stayed out in the car, munching on a fast food chicken sandwich.

"I'm looking for another secretary." Poplin looked at the stacks of papers around him and heaved a sigh. "The committee's past is connected with another group, which preceded them."

Poplin grabbed yet another stick of gum from a half-empty pack on his desk. The fresh scent caused the tingle of a sugar rush through my teeth. "Want one?" Wayne thrust the pack at me. I shook my head.

"As far as the committee is concerned, they have a long

history. And a few odd turns." His chews kept coming at a fast pace forcing the lines in his forehead to bunch up.

"I want it all, Wayne. What can you tell me?"

"You didn't hear it from me, okay?"

"No problem."

"Do you know where all the players were before this committee was formed?" Poplin's voice had an inviting tone of curiosity.

"Where?"

"Remember, I said I'm not going to do all your work. Take a look at some old subcommittee notes regarding counterfeiting. And see if some familiar names pop up."

"Priscomb?"

"Bingo. When he was a senator, he chaired the subcommittee overseeing the Secret Service matters on counterfeiting."

"So what does this have to do with his daughter?"

"Maybe nothing. But maybe his past put his daughter in danger."

"How?"

"I'm not going to point fingers, but the senator has a few enemies."

"Jackels and the summit committee insist their work has nothing to do with her death, and I'm including the senator's past."

"And you trust them?"

"You already know the answer to that."

"I'm just saying," Poplin said, "take a good look at the senator's past and see where it takes you." Poplin glanced toward his computer screen. He pushed a mouse around until he clicked on a page of numbers. "I've got to go over my invoices. You've got enough."

"Wayne. Just a bit more. Why did—"

"You're on your own. That's it. I don't want you to think of me as a source. If you really have to quote someone, you can tell people I told you. I don't care. But just remember, I'm trying to do business with the committee."

"Are you part of the summit?"

"Not yet. They haven't made a final list of vendors and

PR firms. I'm bidding to handle all the press releases. Everything. And they still haven't picked a site. Lane's death will only slow them down."

I could see numbers scroll up on Poplin's screen. The floor squeaked as I approached the door.

Now it was my turn to work a computer mouse. I logged onto the Internet and waited. Mike Brendon had a phone nestled to his ear. Ike leaned up against a chair in the edit room to spot-check the twenty minutes of video, including the interview at the police station.

More than twenty mouse clicks, a few browser searches, and three web-page links later, I found myself at the government subcommittee web site, complete with minutes. Brendon approached.

"Miami wants to know if you've got anything new."

"Other than what we had on the noon . . . nothing."

Brendon squinted at my computer screen. "I don't want to question what you're doing . . . but this is?"

"Research."

"Research?"

"Research."

"Okay. Care to share what that *research* might be? Like a lead story?"

"Not yet. It's too early." I picked up the telephone. "You want me to call Miami? I can tell them myself, because there's just not a lot going on. Jerry Redmond is under wraps by his attorney. The cops aren't talking. Priscomb won't speak for now, and I've got a call into the medical examiner's office. If, and I mean if they are ready to talk, then we've got a new peg for the afternoon."

"Okay. I'll tell Miami you're working on . . . things."

Brendon stepped away. He walked past the row of high-tech scanners. Each one was programmed to get police and fire calls. A constant chatter of cop talk peppered the air. I scrolled the computer screen down until I locked on a US House bio link, and stopped at Priscomb. Everyone in Congress, it seemed, past and present, had a web page.

Born in Tallahassee, the biography listed Priscomb's history, going back to college and earning a degree in accounting. Priscomb's background included a short stint as a mayor's aide before running for the senate. He won the first time, and was reelected to a second term, finally retiring two years ago. The web page failed to mention his brief attempt at a run for the presidency. And only a two-paragraph reference to the subcommittee's work.

"Mike, whose the guy we have in Washington?" I yelled over the squelch of scanner noise.

"Grogan. Jules Grogan. You need the number?"

"Shout it out."

I dialed and got a recording. I left a message and dialed Cat's number.

"Hello."

"Cat? Stacy needs your help." I kept the alarm out of my voice.

"Something wrong?"

"It's not major. Someone tried to jimmy her lock at the hotel. She's coming over to stay with you tonight."

"I knew something was wrong. I came home early and the whole time I kept thinking about her."

I could sense the apprehension building in her voice.

"I'm going to drop by her hotel and she'll follow me over to your place. She can't remember the route."

"Was any other door tampered with?" Cat said. I could hear child voices in the background.

"As far as we know . . . it was just her door."

Cat remained silent. The faint background voices became louder. Shauna was fussing about getting homework done. Cat's voice became a whisper. "What do you make of this? I mean . . . is she okay?"

"It's probably just a hotel thief making the rounds. We'll be by later."

I hung up. Mike held a phone in the air. "I've got Washington." Mike pressed a few buttons and my extension rang.

"Matt here."

"What do you need?" Jules Grogan did not have a standard television voice. It was high-pitched and when he got excited it went even higher.

"I'm checking on someone who left the senate a couple of years ago. What can you tell me about John Priscomb?"

"I just heard his daughter was killed. What a shame. What do you want to know? At the end of his fling for the White House, he hated our guts."

"The reason?"

"The group of reporters who followed him at the time, well, we would listen to his speech, and it was the same old speech, over and over. We used to wear those cheap noise makers around our necks. You know the type? They were metal and when you squeezed those clackers, they sounded like frogs. Whenever he went into his attack on counterfeiters, we heard it so often, we all rebelled and started clacking at the back of the room." Jules laughed until his voice pitched up and out of range.

"What about his staff? Did a Stacy Gaines work for him then?"

"Gaines? Let me think. Don't think so. All I remember is the jerk who was his press secretary. The guy got so angry at us one day, he yanked a noise maker off one of the reporters. It took three of us to break up the fight."

"Jules, I just wanted to get some information on—"

"Wait. I'm trying to remember that guy's name? He wore suits that were too big for him. Like it made him bigger somehow."

I could hear Grogan's loud finger snap over the phone. "This guy went on to a big gig. The word is Priscomb got him appointed. In fact, he's the man running the summit committee. Their executive director. Jackels. That's it. William Jackels."

Chapter Fifteen

The leaves of a black olive tree were kicked up by a breeze and swirled across the parking lot in a rolling clatter until they collected near the door of the Shell Bay Hotel. Twenty-foot sections of the front wall reflected the original peach color, but years of summer blister scorched patches of the stucco to a chalky hue. Operators of the Shell Bay it seemed, didn't spend much on paint or a good security system.

I stood outside waiting for Stacy Gaines. She decided to follow me to where Cat lived. My report for the five o'clock newscast ran about ninety seconds and I was rerunning the story in my mind to see how I could have improved the script.

Stacy pressed fingers on glass and failed to budge the hotel door. She dropped her hand, and pushed a shoulder into the letters S-B-H on the door and stepped into the Florida evening. She didn't approach me. Instead, Stacy waved at me then got behind the wheel of her rental car. Another line of wind-blown, dust-coated leaves rammed against my loafers. I got into the Beemer, drove off, and checked the Chevy Cavalier in my rearview mirror.

We joined the westward march of homebound cars. They spewed out of downtown Fort Lauderdale, headed to pockets of suburbia. Subdivisions, protected by guard gates, and tall walls.

I flipped the visor down and squinted at the final burn of

an amber sunset. The daytime glow of a crimson-streaked sky, dimmed to charcoal in the dusk. I stopped just outside the driveway, to let Stacy pull in first. My Beemer came to a stop, just short of Stacy's rear bumper. Cat's green van took up the other spot. As usual, every window at Cat's one-story home was open.

"Stacy?" Cat's voice filtered through the window screens.

Stacy shouted, as she removed the seat belt and pushed the car door.

"I'm all right."

We stepped into the house to a mix of smells. Shauna sat on the floor applying something to her hair. The flavor of cooked sausage came from the kitchen.

"I've got plenty in there," Cat pointed, but her eyes stayed on Stacy. We followed Cat and the aroma trail.

"You staying?" The question came from Jason. Stacy smiled and shrugged her shoulders.

"Did you finish what I told you?" There was a firmness in Cat's voice. Jason's inquisitive expression melted into a smile.

"Well . . . did you?" Cat asked again.

"Did what?" The four-year-old appeared to be stalling to find the right answer.

"I told him to clean up his room . . . guests were coming." Cat's words were directed at the cupboard as she pulled down two plates. Jason and his smile were gone by the time Cat turned around to line up the plates on the glass table.

"I know what you're thinking, Cat." Stacy folded and unfolded the thin fingers in her lap. "I'm letting Lane's death freak me out. But I just need some time away from the hotel."

Cat scraped the last of the sausage, peppers and vegetables onto the plates. "That had to be a random thing."

"What can you tell me about Jackels and Priscomb?" I sliced up the meat and waited.

"Is this the reporter talking or a friend?" Cat glared at me.

"Both." I took refuge in the food, drawing a fork to my mouth, while waiting to be banished from the table.

"It's okay Cat, I'll answer him. You mean because they worked together in Washington?"

"Exactly. How did Jackels end up running the summit committee?"

"He was appointed." Stacy paused for a moment. "That's not quite right. Priscomb recommended Jackels for the job. You have to remember, I wasn't in the picture then. I came a bit later."

Cat walked the silent pace of a mother checking the activities of a child. She leaned into the hallway toward Jason's room, then returned to sit at the table.

The food was so good, I didn't want to interrupt the ritual of nourishment to the body, but I kept up the flow of questions. "So Jackels gets appointed and then he hires Priscomb's daughter?"

"You make it sound like some dirty-bag job." Stacy pushed the plate away. Cat's eyes took aim at me again.

"I'm just trying to get a picture of all the players and how this committee got formed. So you applied to Jackels?"

"Lane hired me." Stacy pushed her fingers into her eyes and rubbed in small circles. "They're going to fly her body up to Tallahassee in a few days. The funeral will be up there. Senator Priscomb I think will stay around for awhile to see how this investigation goes." Stacy dropped her hands, revealing tear-rimmed eyes. She pulled the plate back into position and picked up a fork. "I really miss Lane." Stacy talked into the plate.

Cat walked over and gave Stacy a hug. "First time I met her, I was feeding her," Cat said. "Remember that?"

Stacy's lips bent at the edges in the smallest of smiles. "Cat plucked me right off the campus. Felt sorry for me, took me home and fed me."

Cat's hands formed around an imaginary person. "Her waist was that big around. Stacy looked like she hadn't eaten in days."

"I spent so much time in class, then studying, I didn't have time to eat. Or the money." Stacy's fork poked at the food on the plate. "If it wasn't for Cat, I think I would have just shriveled up."

"I didn't mind. We had plenty." Cat leaned against the kitchen counter.

Stacy put down her fork, then wiped a tear to the side of her face. "Lane was the same way. Seems like we were always trying to take care of each other. And since Cat left to move back south . . ."

"You almost didn't let me leave Atlanta." Cat's head tilted with a certain purpose, almost in mock sarcasm. "Told me that she was going to stop me from putting my bags in the car."

A smile finally moved across Stacy's face. "I didn't have many friends. Cat dropped out of college, pregnant. And I lost my running buddy. When Cat moved down here with her mother, I felt lost. Until Lane arrived." Stacy's glance locked with ours. We ate in silence for the next few minutes until Stacy reached into her purse, searching for something. Finally she jumped up from the table.

"I left my briefcase in the car. I need something to show you . . . be right back." The jingle of car keys softened as she stepped away from us. I stood up to check if there was any cake left.

"Matt!" Stacy's voice carried through the house. Urgent and direct. Cat beat me to the front door. We looked out into the driveway. A single streetlight emitted a soft glow. Stacy stood in the shadows, holding her car keys.

"My briefcase is open!" she screamed. "Someone broke into the car!"

Chapter Sixteen

T wo round faces appeared at the door. "Get back in the house, now!" Cat yelled. Jason and Shauna withdrew from the doorway. The blinds parted and they pressed their noses against the window.

I looked around for any cars or someone running off. Nothing. Just the regular array of cars parked for the night. I checked on my Beemer. Windows and doors intact. I reached into my glove box and pulled out a flashlight. I directed the beam at the window of Stacy's rental car.

"Who would do that?" Cat's voice was a notch below desperation.

We inspected the driver's side door. "Looks like someone jimmied the door," I said. "Take a look." There was a small scratch on the window probably from the flat metal bar used to open car doors. The door was still ajar. "We must have been followed."

I could see the anxiety in Stacy's face. First the hotel door, now the car. She threaded a hand through her hair. The briefcase remained in the car, open. Sheets of paper were on the seat and the floor.

I walked around the car and checked the other door. "Did you notice anyone behind you when we drove out here?"

"No. Just a bunch of car lights. You can't notice faces."

"I'll call the police and get them to check for prints," I said.

"No police." Stacy was adamant.

"You might want to rethink that . . . they can look for car marks, knock on some doors, talk to some neighbors . . ."

"No police!"

"Why call the police?" Now Cat was backing up Stacy.

I stepped to the front door and stood in front of Cat.

"The windows are open, but I didn't hear anything. What about you?"

Cat shook her head.

I approached the Cavalier, crouched, and directed the flashlight beam under the car. Stacy angled her face to follow the light. "What are you looking for?"

"A device. Perhaps a bomb. Anything."

"Bomb?" Stacy grabbed the light from me and made the beam creep a slow walk toward the muffler, drive shaft and motor mounts.

I tried to reassure her. "I doubt if there's anything there. I just thought I'd check."

"I still don't want the police." Stacy handed the flashlight back to me. "I'm not going against the wishes of Jackels. He made it very clear after the problem at the hotel. I'll report it directly to him."

"I just think we should put in a call to Detective Collins. The person who did this must have been on foot. A car would be too loud. And they worked fast. I still don't understand. If you were going to be attacked, they would just come at you. Someone is making sure this is all very public and they're being very clear about getting your attention. We need to bring in some outside help. Namely, the police."

Cat reached her arm around Stacy. "Matt, stay there. I'll take Stacy inside and call the rental agency. She needs another car."

Stacy walked out of Cat's grip. "I'm not afraid," Stacy said. "I want to work this out internally. And that means I call Jackels. I've got his pager number."

"You're sure about this?" I asked. "I hate to put it this way, but someone could be stalking you. Maybe the same person who attacked Lane."

Stacy wrapped herself by crossing her arms. "We've had enough publicity on this already. One person is dead, and this could just be some teenager out proving his manhood to some friends. No police. Just Jackels."

Cat walked Stacy inside. I checked the street again. I heard the rumble of tires on pavement down the block. A couple of houses away, a garbage can lid hit the ground with a thud. Across the street, a dog barked in reaction. I passed it off as the casual noise of the neighborhood unless the sound in the backyard came from something more sinister. Shauna and Jason were still watching from the window.

"Stay inside," I instructed. "I'll be right back."

I stepped off in the direction of the garbage can. The first home I passed had the lights on, coming from somewhere in the rear of the house. The blinds in the front windows were framed in light. I kept going. The next home was dark. The sounds had to come from here. I kept silent waiting to hear some movement. Moments passed. The yard was surrounded by a wooden fence, shadowbox style. The grass kept my steps quiet. I reached the latch. And waited.

Decision time. If I went inside the yard, it could be considered trespassing. I stood there, slightly bent over waiting for any movement. I grabbed the top of the fence, and pushed up on my toes to look over the edge of the six-foot-tall fence. The light pole was on the other side of the street. I could just make out a few trees, a small walkway and something on the ground.

I reached into my pocket and pulled out the flashlight and aimed the beam. The garbage can lid was on the back door ledge. The plastic bag in the container was open to bits of paper and a thick bundle of leaves. I glanced up at the windows. I wanted to make sure I didn't become a south Florida accident: Reporter shot to death, homeowner thought it was a burglar. Only the faint glint of a few night clouds reflected off the windows.

I eased myself down from the fence. No dogs. I could search the yard. The fence parted and the wooden gate came at me with the force of a fullback smashing into a group of angry faces. Only the face was mine. The jolt knocked me to the ground. Before I had a chance to focus, my right side burned with the pain of someone driving a kick into my ribs. Then another. My hands swung in the direction of the attack to protect my side. Another kick. My breathing came at me in short bursts. I saw flashes of black clothing. No face, just a blur of body motion and a gnarled line of shadows for the nose. There was no definition to the facial features. Eye sockets and cheeks were meshed into a dark covering.

At first I coiled for another barrage of kicks, then I tried to get up swinging. The figure was gone. I could hear the steady beat of footsteps running away until only my coughs echoed in the night air. I tried to take in a breath but I coughed and wheezed while tendrils of pain ripped through my body. I spit into my hands. I could see the glisten of my saliva was free of blood. Maybe it was just a bruise and no internal bleeding. My ribs felt sore but not broken.

Unsteady, but moving, I reached for the flashlight on the ground, then trained the beam on the yard. My breathing became regular but the pain stayed with me, refusing to subside. A small corner near the garbage can must have been the hiding spot. I looked but I couldn't find anything. I walked to the front door of the house and knocked. No answer. By the time I reached Cat's driveway, the soreness was becoming less of a factor. Anger took its place.

"Oh my God! Matt, what happened?" Cat surveyed my body. In the room light, one side of my shirt was out of my pants. Black scuff marks stretched several inches down my right side.

"Someone was out there." This time I didn't wait for Stacy to protest, I dialed homicide. I couldn't reach Detective Collins, but I left a message, then punched nine-one-one and talked to the emergency operator. I dropped the phone back into the cradle.

"They're on the way."

"Who was out there?" I could see the frenzy in Cat's eyes as she reached out to touch the mark on the shirt. I recoiled from her in pain and dropped into a chair.

Stacy raked her hand against the curtains, pulling them to one side and stared into the street. Her bracelets slid down her wrist and jingled into a new position on her arm.

Another wave of pain throbbed through my side. "Whoever it was, he's gone. Long gone. But I'll be all right."

"Where was he?" Cat pulled Shauna and Jason into her. Tight. Shauna kept staring at me.

"Two houses down. Who lives there?"

"Amanda Cerkin and her husband, but they're off visiting their son in Sarasota. That's where he was? In the house?"

"No, the backyard. He was probably watching us from there."

Stacy swept her fingers down her arm as if to scrape an imaginary creature from her body. She slowly eased into a section of the couch.

"Lane's killer." Stacy's words were spoken toward the floor.

"You don't know that," Cat said. She sat down next to Stacy. "It was probably a punk, some thug. Matt probably stopped a burglary."

I checked my watch. Just a few minutes had passed.

"Any word on Jackels?"

"He hasn't answered the page," Stacy said.

Stacy jumped when the phone rang. Cat rushed to catch it before the second ring. "Yes?" She looked around the room. "He's right here." I heard the soft clink of a car gear being put into park. Jason ran to the window.

"There's two cars out there," the four-year-old announced. Cat went to the door, while I reached for the phone.

"Hello?"

"Matt, it's Detective Collins. What's up?"

"I thought I should give you a call on what happened here." I briefed Collins about Stacy's car and the scuffle at the fence. And I mentioned the problem at the hotel. Again, he did a lot of listening without much reaction. A uniform walked into the house. Jason was immediately fascinated with everything shiny on her uni. She had no makeup or fingernail polish. The man who followed her inside was Jackels.

"Look, Collins, the officer is here, so I can give her a statement." I hung up the phone and led the officer back outside. Jackels held his hand out until Stacy eased her palm into his. There was an awkward moment as we stood around trying to figure where to start. Jackels checked Stacy. His eyebrows dropped at the edges, like the first time I saw him at the podium talking about Lane Redmond. The business suit was gone. He wore a jogging outfit, and new sneakers. Jackels looked for something to wipe the sweat from his forehead.

"I'm Officer Kate Parker. Why don't you walk me down to where this happened."

I talked to her as we approached the house, first showing her the car window, then we walked up to the fence and I pointed to the garbage can. Parker pulled out a long black flashlight and checked the yard. A white beam drifted from the garbage can to the fence opening.

The officer studied me. "Did you go into the yard?"

"No. I just peaked over the top. I didn't see anything at first, then when I stepped back, to go to the front door, that's when the fence door came flying at me."

"You get a look?"

I sighed until the pain tore again at my side. "No. I got knocked down, and he started kicking . . . when I looked up, it was just dark. But he was wearing something on his face . . . a mask."

"Could you tell it was a man?"

"I'm sure about that."

"They took off in that direction?" Officer Parker pointed toward the state road. I nodded.

"And you think this might be related to the homicide Collins is working and the hotel room?" Her words were directed toward the yard.

"I'll leave that up to him. I just wanted to let him know about the car and what happened."

Parker started jotting something on a pad. Between questions, she kept adjusting her police radio. She spent several minutes talking with Stacy. We again inspected the car.

Before leaving, she dusted the Cavalier. The black powder made small dust clouds as she applied the brush. She applied a tape and lifted a few prints, and made some more notes.

"Thanks. Detective Collins will be in touch."

Across the street, a neighbor glanced through the spread curtains, then closed them up. Parker tossed the pad in her car, and left. When I reached the front door, Stacy and Jackels were getting ready to leave.

"Thanks for looking out for her. I'll get her to a different hotel." Jackels turned his head in the direction of Stacy's car. "You gonna be all right, waiting for the locksmith?"

"Sure. What hotel?"

"The Whitestone. It's a mile up Federal Highway."

Jackels eased Stacy into his black Benz. He shut the door, then stopped in front of me. "You okay? I heard you took quite a kick?"

"I'll be fine. Have you been working out?"

"I do a little running."

"Oh . . . not too far?"

"Nearby," he said.

"You just seemed to work up a good sweat in that air-conditioned car."

He ignored me.

"Did you tell Stacy not to get the police involved?"

"So what if I did?"

"Why?"

"Listen, Matt. This is none of your concern."

"Did you tell Lane Redmond not to call the police?"

"This is none of your business—"

"Did you convince her to keep quiet about someone following her?"

He paused. "I didn't believe her at first. I just thought it was for the good of the summit conference to keep it low-profile."

"So you told her to keep quiet about a stalker? She had no one to rely on. That's why she called me."

Nothing from Jackels.

"And now she's dead."

His eyebrows formed an arch over eyes fixed in a glare.

But it lasted for the length of a blink. The rigid cracks at the edges of his gravel-gray eyes eased back into a calm demeanor. The eyebrows flattened. Jackels ran his hand over his forehead.

"One more thing. What about Lane's father?" I asked. "Does he have some old enemies who should be investigated? Maybe there's a connection?"

"Leave him out of this," Jackels said.

"For Stacy's sake, can't you take a look at this?"

"Always the questions." He reached for his keys, and positioned himself at the steering wheel. The Benz eased down the street, silent as a stare.

"I've got the rental agency on the phone," Cat said. I turned around to see her at the door. "He'll be here in fifteen minutes."

"No problem," I said. "I'll wait."

Chapter Seventeen

I spent the night on the couch, guarding the door at Cat's urging, listening for any rustling outside. It remained quiet and I didn't wake up until the pointed finger of a four-year-old jabbed me in the nose.

"Morning," I whispered.

Jason looked at me with the wonderment of a scientist studying his first piece of moon rock. He was dressed and ready for preschool. I eased up to a sitting position and started to rub my face but stopped. The pain still throbbed at my side.

Jason retreated to the kitchen where the clang of a spoon on a bowl of cereal must have caused his stomach juices to stir. I eased into the kitchen. Cat surveyed me.

"I don't want to tell you what you look like."

"I know. I called the office last night . . . told them I was going to be late."

"You okay?"

"I'm fine."

"You never went in for x-rays or anything."

"I'm fine."

Cat stood at the sink wiping down the counter top. Through the kitchen window, the morning wind jerked at the fronds of a grouping of queen palm trees. Jason let his spoon drop into the bowl after each mouthful. Shauna got up from the table to leave.

"Did you forget something?" Cat's question made Shauna's chin drop. The eight-year-old stepped back to the table and picked up the empty bowl. A soft rinse washed out the milk and then Shauna placed the bowl and spoon into the dishwasher.

"Thank you," Cat said. No response from Shauna.

Cat wore a white blouse with a forest-green and red-checked jacket, solid green pants and black pumps. A hint of the morning sun reflected against her eyes. Her stare at the window lingered.

"Are you thinking about Stacy?" I asked.

"Yes." Cat pulled her gaze from the window, the intensity of her eyes directed at me. "What a welcome to south Florida."

"But at least she's got you to count on."

"I hope so." Cat watched Shauna and Jason pack lunches and book bags. When he walked by, she tucked in the back of his shirt.

"Mom," he moaned, shrugging off the helping hand from Cat. She looked at me as if I was being added to her list of last-minute inspections.

"I've got a busy day and I need to get away from the bank and get over to the library," Cat started. "If you find out anything about Stacy, get in touch with me right away, okay?"

I nodded.

Cat turned as if she wanted to add one last detail. "I have a test for my course, then I'm going to try and call Stacy after that, but knowing her, I won't be able to reach her."

I nodded again and left. A half-raised arm was all I could offer as a good-bye and I pulled out of the driveway. I had to get home and shower. Stacy's car was still there. I eased my Beemer past the fence a few doors away and thought about the intruder in the dark.

Chapter Eighteen

I was in the office just minutes and my phone rang. I caught it on the third ring.

"Bowens."

"Hey Matt, it's your man in DC. I've been doing some more checking on the committee."

"Sure. What do you have?"

"Take this for what you want, but there was going to be a senate investigation into campaign funding but it never got off the ground." His cell phone wavered in and out.

"Who was the target?"

"Priscomb. It seems it had something to do with campaign donations. There was talk of an independent counsel to be appointed by the Attorney General but it died about the same time as the rumors started." His voice was clear again.

I tried to write down details as fast as his words came at me. "That has to be right about the time he dropped out of the presidential run. Wasn't more done on this?"

"Media wise? No. There was a closed door session and no one talked. This is all I could get."

"Where did the dirty money come from?"

"That's going to be your job. The person who would know retired down there. She once worked on Priscomb's staff. Her name is Shirley Belcamp."

More notes, more details. I circled the name Belcamp three times.

"When Priscomb dropped out of the race, what did he give for a reason?" I flipped to a fresh page on my pad.

"There were all kinds of reasons. His wife's health for one. We never questioned it because he dropped out so early. He was a non-factor. We moved on."

"Thanks."

I searched the phone books, directory assistance, and tax records on the Internet, but found no Shirley Belcamp. Ike arrived but stayed for only a few minutes before Mike sent him out to a location to check out whether a car smashed through the front of a clothing shop.

I could have used a computer service called the BodyTracer to find Belcamp, but decided to work a bit harder first. I went back to an older set of phone books and found seven listings for Belcamp. I picked up the phone and started dialing each one. I reached three voice mail machines and a disconnected phone line. The fifth time a woman's voice answered.

"Excuse me, but I'm trying to reach a Shirley Belcamp."

I heard a bird in the background along with a television turned up a bit too much.

"Who wants to know?"

"My name is Matt Bowens, with Channel Fourteen news. I'm doing a follow-up story on the death of Lane Redmond, and I'm looking for a Shirley Bel—"

"I'm Shirley Belcamp."

I jammed the phone up against my ear. Her voice was low and the bird and television were working against me.

"I'm trying to reach people who knew Lane Redmond, to get a better picture of what she was like."

"I really don't talk to reporters."

"It wouldn't take much of your time. Anything would be helpful, a picture, a story about her."

The bird stopped and there was a pause. From the television, a loud conversation between a talk show host and some rowdy guests reduced in volume until I thought the phone line went dead. "You still there?" I asked.

"Yes."

"The listing says Ray Belcamp . . ."

"I lost Ray last year. Just never had them change the listing into my name."

"Is it okay if I stop by to talk to you?"

"Listen, I've had dealings with reporters. You say one thing and it gets all twisted."

"How long did you work for Priscomb?"

Her long sigh was an answer by itself. I imagined her in the middle of scrapes with lobbyists, condominium managers who controlled thousands of votes, and a determined media.

"I was in charge of his staff the entire time he held office."

"Again, is it okay if we talk?"

"No camera, and we can talk."

I parked my Beemer behind a Mercedes Benz station wagon. The once shiny Benz was now a flat beige, bleached by the sun without enough pigment to reflect my white shirt. The outside of the house looked like it was rolled with a fresh coat of bone-white paint. Rows of red Impatiens lined the walkway. A mahogany door opened before I could knock.

"Come on in." Shirley Belcamp was older than I figured. She wore her hair swept back and she had a high forehead. A parrot stood on a perch off to the left. We kept going until we reached the family room.

"I watch you on television," she said, sinking into a chair.

"Thank you."

"I don't trust reporters. Not a one of 'em. But I've seen your work. And I like it."

"If you've been burned in the past, the only thing I can say is judge me by my stories, and decide if I'm fair."

She reached over to a table then handed me a folder.

"How long have you been retired?" I asked.

"It's just been a few months now. They had to push me out

of the office." She stopped in front of a row of photographs on a bookshelf. "The picture is right there."

"I'll return it to you."

"We took that picture just after her twenty-second birthday. She was so happy." The lines around her smile bent upward. "She was just out of college, and everything seemed so right."

"And her husband?"

"I never liked him. You know sometimes you just can't convince a person somebody is wrong for them. Her friend couldn't even—"

"Who was that?"

"They were close. Even though they came from different sides of Atlanta. I forget her name . . . Sarah . . . or something."

"Stacy?"

"That's it. Stacy Gaines."

"Stacy is down here now."

Belcamp pressed her hands into her face, pulling back across her cheeks until the wrinkles momentarily disappeared, only to return as soon as she removed her fingers.

"Is she okay?"

"I want to say yes, but I think someone is following her."

"Oh my."

"She's in good hands, but I wanted to ask you about something else." I measured my words, fully aware that I was venturing into a sensitive area. "I'm trying to find out if the investigation of Senator Priscomb had anything to do with Lane's death."

"There was no investigation." Her words were tight, defensive and final. She glanced at the folder as if she wanted to take it back. "I think our conversation is about over. It was a pleasure."

"The only reason I brought it up is because another life might be at stake. I don't want anything to happen to Stacy."

"Do the police have a suspect?"

"No. There's a lot of speculation, but no real connections to the murder."

Her eyes blinked until they were moist. "Did you talk to Mr. Priscomb about this?"

"Not yet. I was hoping to get some answers before I talked with him."

"Give me some time to think about it."

A stack of pink telephone messages were tucked under the phone on my desk. One from Ramirez, the news director. There was one from Cat, a note from Stacy Gaines, and a message from John Priscomb.

"Our DC man had this expressed overnight." Mike Brendon handed me a folder filled with Washington area newspaper articles about Priscomb. "See if you've got a lead story in that stack of messages, we could use one."

I called Ramirez first, but I was told he was in with the general manager of the TV station. I dialed the number for Priscomb. No answer.

I looked through the articles, searching for names connected with the investigation. Priscomb was never quoted or interviewed, but four names kept resurfacing. I tapped the keyboard and logged onto the Internet and entered the names. Two people mentioned were not in a position to donate money to the campaign. I researched a third name only to find he went into local government out west. And that left me with the name of Hector Colon. I flipped through my Rolodex and picked up the phone.

Chapter Nineteen

Michael Ivory looked at my briefcase as if his years inspecting bags at the airport were not over. His eyes never blinked until I pulled out my pad.

Ivory checked his watch. "I can't promise I can keep everything on the record."

I hated the direction of his comment and I didn't want to let him hide behind an excuse to stop talking. "Thanks for squeezing us in."

Again Ivory peered at his wrist.

"I just wanted to catch you before your luncheon," I told him. "Tell me everything you can about Hector Colon."

Ivory's chest swelled with a deep breath. He was tall, with enough muscle mass to show he still worked out. He kept his afro haircut short. I first met him during a sting at the airport, conducting surveillance for baggage thieves. During his stay with the airport division of the police department, Ivory racked up arrests, busting drug mules, and pickpockets until he took the position of spokesman for the US Attorney's office in south Florida. Ike adjusted the camera and gave me a nod meaning the camera was on and recording.

"Again, about Hector Colon."

"As we sit here, authorities are still looking for Hector Colon. He is well known in the counterfeiting world and worked out of a base in South America. Our attention has always been on illegal drugs but Colon always managed to do something to get our attention."

For the next few minutes, Ivory gave me the history of Colon's past, ending with the plot of how he managed to escape federal agents.

"Six months ago, Colon was tied to a shipment of one million dollars in counterfeit bills. He was indicted, but remains at large."

"He's been connected to deaths?" My question made Ivory pause as if to inventory another area of Colon's deeds.

"He's been connected to the deaths of three people in his organization. We can't disclose all the reasons why the men were murdered, but the person responsible for losing the shipment was among the dead."

"And this same man is believed to have donated to the campaign of John Priscomb?"

He paused. "Now you're getting into areas that are beyond the scope of our investigation. Remember, that happened while Colon was still very new to us. I can tell you that we have been following his actions and yes, some very real money did go to a number of campaigns, but we should add, once it was discovered where the money was coming from, the committees for those candidates returned the proceeds and contacted the authorities."

I went down my mental list of questions. "Are you cooperating with other agencies to see if Hector Colon could be responsible for the death of Lane Redmond?"

"I can't answer that directly, but if an agency calls us, we cooperate."

"Are organizers of the summit under protection because of Colon?"

"As you know, I'm not a part of the security team for the summit, but if called, we would provide any assistance or information, but beyond that, I can't get into security procedures."

"Is Hector Colon in the United States?"

"We're not certain of his whereabouts."

"And Colon is capable of—?"

"Mr. Colon is capable of drug trafficking, counterfeit operations and murder."

When I failed to ask another question, Ike stopped the camera and unsnapped it from the tripod. He stepped off and recorded a few setup shots, then packed his gear away.

"Is any of this going to make air?" Ike uttered the question as he packed the tripod and camera into the van.

"Not yet. I don't have a clear connection to Lane Redmond. At least not yet. I just wanted to get the interview in the can. It will become useful at some point."

"And the senator?" Ike asked.

"If Priscomb angered Colon somehow, maybe he had Lane killed. It's a remote angle right now, but I've got to pursue it."

Now it was Ike who stared at his watch. "Lunch? If we don't take it Matt, we may never see food." Ike pointed the van into the traffic. My beeper tapped at my side. I glanced at the number and picked up the cell phone.

"Mike?"

"Where are you guys?" There was an urgency in Mike Brendon's voice.

"We're just leaving our interview."

"Head to Fort Lauderdale. John Priscomb called. He's ready to talk."

Chapter Twenty

The elevator door opened to a wide lobby of leather chairs and a large window view of the intracoastal waterway. The law office of McGreen and Campbell took up the entire twenty-ninth floor. A secretary pointed us in the direction of a conference room. Ike set up the camera, and pointed the lens toward a sedate section of the room with a wall of legal books as a backdrop.

John Priscomb entered the room holding a rolled up paper. His white shirt was tieless and unbuttoned, showing tufts of gray chest hair. Priscomb nodded hello rather than speak. His wife Para followed, her head tilted down. She glanced once at the camera and sat down next to Priscomb. He placed his hand over her trembling fingers then pulled his hand away to gesture as he spoke.

"I want you to know that the reason we're agreeing to do this is to find out who did this." His voice was thick with rage. Priscomb sounded more like a man ready to release the formal trappings of a politician and take up the burning spirit of a father set on retaliation.

"Let me know when you're ready." Priscomb shifted in his seat.

Ike looked up from his eyepiece and gave a motion to ask a question.

"What is it you want to say?" I said.

Priscomb looked at his wife for a moment before looking

past me and directly into the camera. "We know someone out there has the vital information to help police find a suspect. We are prepared to offer a reward of five hundred thousand dollars for any information leading to the arrest and conviction of the person responsible for Lane's death."

The mention of Lane's name caused Para to reach for a handkerchief. She dabbed at her eyes then held her head up for the first time since she walked into the room. Her eyes were edged in tears. Priscomb unfurled the paper in his hand.

"I have established a hotline for anyone to call if you have information. You don't have to leave your name but someone is there to take down your information, twenty-four hours a day."

Priscomb spoke the numbers and I took down the listing.

"This person stalked, and killed our daughter. Please, if someone saw or heard anything, please pick up the phone."

"There's still so much we don't know about her," I began. "Tell me about Lane."

"She was the kind of person who would stop and help you even if she didn't know you. She did volunteer work for the homeless in Atlanta. She had a sense of humor, and placed her friends above everything."

I took my time before my next question. "Do you think her death had anything to do with her work on the summit committee?"

Priscomb rolled up the paper again in his hand. He waved it in the air like a baseball bat. "We have nothing before us to show her work had anything to do with this. She was not in law enforcement and there was no reason why anyone should target her."

"Have police singled out the names of any suspects?"

"No. Not at this time. You have to understand, they can only tell us so much."

"Have you mentioned to them to check out the name of Hector Colon?"

The rolled up paper came down on Priscomb's leg with a soft whack. "That name has only come up once in my life.

It was dealt with, and it's not a factor in this case. I resent that question, and I would kindly ask that you pursue matters which pertain to this case."

"But could a man as dangerous as Colon target Lane—"

"I know you have been talking to my former staff members . . . Mrs. Belcamp. She told me that you're digging up some angle about my presidential campaign. Again, there is nothing to connect Hector Colon to anything with this case. And in my daughter's death, I don't want to speculate. We need facts and we need a phone call."

I waited before posing another question, letting the silence between us build. The handkerchief in Para's hand dropped to her lap. "Don't you think we've thought about that?" Her eyes narrowed.

"Did she talk to you about who might be stalking her?" I asked.

Para closed her grip, drawing her fingers together. Frustration built up in her voice. Her words carried far beyond the decorum of a politician's wife, to levels of crackling anger. "If I could, I would find this person. I would track him down myself."

Priscomb reached over and again put his hand over her fist. She relaxed her fingers. "I just want justice."

I let her words end the interview. Priscomb handed me the paper with the hotline number. "Hopefully someone will call," he said. "This is hard on us but we just ask one thing. Don't let this end here. We're hoping your station will let you do more stories. It's uncomfortable for us, but if there's no news coverage, Lane's death is forgotten and a witness might not be convinced to come forward."

I folded the paper and tucked it in my suit pocket. "I brought up Colon because of his past. And to be honest, his possible connection to this case. Is there a number to reach you?"

Priscomb reached for my reporter pad and jotted some numbers. "It's the inside number to the law office. They can get hold of me, day or night." He pulled his suit together, and looked back as if to search my mind, probably wondering how much I knew about Colon. "I can understand how a reporter would delve into Colon's background, but I don't think it has any bearing on Lane's death."

Ike closed the van door and leveled a question. "So how much are we going to dwell on Hector Colon?"

I reached for the cell phone before answering. "Not at all. For now. Unless I can directly tie him into the homicide and Priscomb directly, I can't mention him. The time will come when I can use the info." A secretary in the homicide office answered the phone.

"Is Detective Collins in?"

"No, they're on the road." The voice came back flat and detached. "Do you want to leave a message on voice mail?"

"Yes, that's fine." I left a plea for Collins to call, then I started hitting phone numbers again. Frank Walker answered on the first ring. "Police information office, Walker speaking."

"This is Matt Bowens. Collins is on the road. I've got a name to throw at you."

"Go ahead."

"Is homicide looking at a counterfeiter named Hector Colon?"

I could sense he was writing down the name. "You say Colon?"

"Colon, first name Hector. He's wanted on unrelated murder charges in South America, and he faces a major bogus money indictment in the States. See if that name has surfaced."

"No problem. They can give me an answer but I might not be able to pass it on to you."

Walker was about to give me the dreaded phrase. The comment intended to protect a probe, while killing a story, forcing reporters to use sources.

"You know how it is Matt. If Colon's name becomes part of the investigation, I may not be able to say anything."

Once he hung up, I was dialing again. This time to Mike Brendon.

"Yes?"

"Listen Mike, Priscomb is putting up five hundred thousand of his own money for a reward. His wife spoke as well. Tell the producers I think I have their lead story."

Chapter Twenty-one

A line of black-edged shapes served as clouds. Ripples of intracoastal water kept turning darker shades of blue with the evening slide of the sun into the skyline. Mike Brendon walked past the window of the news bureau.

"Did you ever talk to Ramirez?"

Channel 14's news director didn't like to wait long for reporters to respond. "I talked to him. He wants me to take over the spot doing consumer reporting."

"And you told him?" Brendon asked.

"I told him I don't want it. I'm happy doing what I'm doing."

Brendon turned his gaze to the window. "How long is your story?" Brendon pulled his right hand through the strands of beard.

"Over two minutes." I dialed Cat's number. It rang six times before the answer machine finally kicked on and I left a message.

"They should have led the show with your story." Brendon stopped stroking the beard, crossed his arms, and watched the monitors. On Channel Fourteen, the lead story was switched from my interview with Priscomb to the rescue of an alligator caught in a storm drain just yards from a row of homes. During the year, and especially during mating season, alligators showed up everywhere.

"Pictures of an alligator always get their attention," I

yelled. The trapper pulled the gator out of the hole tail first. The animal's huge jaws were kept in check by tightly rolled duct tape around its mouth.

"Alligators. Coming to a neighborhood near you." Brendon's smile was barely visible through the whiskers. He removed his glasses and wiped them clean of the day's filth. Brendon pushed the glasses back into place.

Exactly two minutes and twelve seconds later, south Florida watched John Priscomb plead for eyewitnesses. Throughout the story, Ike put in the newest picture of Lane Redmond given to us by Shirley Belcamp. There were tight shots of Priscomb holding his wife's hand. When it was over, the toll-free number was put on the screen for several seconds along with the regular police crime hotline.

"Homicide should love us for getting their number out there." Brendon moved past the huge window, never looking out at the changing hues of bay water.

"What homicide really loves is a closed case," I said. "How's the diet?"

Brendon released the bulk of the pent-up air in his chest, sighing so loudly Ike stepped out of his edit booth. The wastebasket in the corner was topped with paper. Brendon picked up the basket and tipped it toward me to reveal balled up burger wrappers and a pizza box. "Does that answer your question?" Brendon shouted. "Didn't last two days. The diet isn't the problem. It's me. I was born to eat."

I wanted to wait awhile at my desk to see if Cat would call back or if Collins finally came back from his stint on the road. Fifteen minutes later, I gave up.

Chapter Twenty-two

"This is the perfect location." Stacy never stayed in one spot. She kept turning and talking, aiming her words at the draped windows and pointing out the marble countertop. "I just need you to do me one favor and check out the doors and locks."

"I'm really not a security expert but I'll take a look."

Stacy gave up on the hotel room and found a two-bedroom house. She asked for help to look over the place. Cat had a friend watch the kids.

"You could use a few items," I started. "A few bucks at the hardware store and some tools and it should be a lot better."

"Thanks for coming. I saw your report on the reward money," Stacy said.

"Five hundred thousand is a lot of money. If that doesn't motivate somebody . . ."

Stacy reached into her purse. "There's something I want you to see." She pulled out an envelope and tugged gently at a photograph. "Remember the night my car was damaged?"

Cat nodded. Stacy handed the picture to Cat.

"This is what I was going to get from my car." We looked at the photograph of Stacy standing next to Lane Redmond.

"I was on the job, working for the committee for just a few days when that picture was taken." Stacy let out a deep breath. "I wish I could go back to that moment."

Stacy stepped into the kitchen and pulled out a tray from the oven. The smell of cooked pizza filled up the kitchen. Stacy reached for the plates. Cat was still admiring the photograph.

I pulled up a stool to the countertop. "How did you find this place?"

"Jackels knew somebody who wanted a house sitter. It's all mine until they come back."

"Is it all right if I drill holes?" I asked.

"Sure. I just can't change the locks."

"Actually, that was the first thing I was going to recommend."

"Can't do it. The owners would be in shock if they came back and found the locks are different."

"Wouldn't you rather be around people? In a hotel?" Cat asked.

Stacy looked around the room. "This reminds me of the place I had in Atlanta. I think I told you Lane helped me find it. I just feel secure in a house. I don't care what anyone thinks, I prefer this over a hotel room."

"Stacy, in those days before Lane . . ." I stopped, trying to come up with another word for murder. "Were you on good terms with her?"

"Why, is that something the police told you?"

"No. But I was wondering—"

Stacy bunched up her brow. Cat's eyes narrowed to thin slits. She eased a slice of pizza onto a plate and placed the food down hard in front of me so the sound echoed off the green and white wallpaper.

"If you don't want to talk about this . . ."

"No. That's okay." Stacy started to rub her nose and drew her hands across her face as if to wipe away the thoughts about Lane's death. "Lane stopped returning my calls. She said very little in the office."

"Why?"

Stacy paused. "About two weeks before they found her, she told me about somebody following her."

"And you convinced her to call the police?"

"I convinced her . . ." Tears formed at the corners of her eyes. "I was following Jackels' lead and told her it was probably nothing. I should have listened to her. And then, when I found out her husband was in town, I was sure it was Jerry."

"Let me be honest about why I'm asking. When Lane called me, I wondered why someone with so many contacts to federal authorities couldn't go to you, or Jackels?"

"We all let her down. We told her she was being paranoid. To forget about it." Stacy looked out at the open part of the room, speaking to no one in particular.

"That's enough Matt." One look at Cat's expression and I was finished asking questions. The food became the topic. Lane's conversation, short as it was, kept turning in my mind until Cat looked at her watch. "Got to get back. The baby-sitter will be looking for me."

Stacy walked us to the door. "Thanks for coming. I feel so much safer now."

Chapter Twenty-three

I started my morning at the office of Suspect Watch. The place was stuck in one corner of the police department, with just enough space for a telephone and someone to take in tips from the public on assaults, rapes, and murders. One thousand dollars to the tipster if there was an arrest and conviction. The death of Lane Redmond was a high-profile case. Nick Spender, the commander of the unit, usually took the night taking in calls after the broadcast of a reward appeal.

A photograph of Nick's family, a calendar, and a thick writing pad were the only things on his desk. The walls and metal filing cabinets were covered with flyers. Murder victims and people missing for months or years. Lane's picture had a place near Spender's desk.

"Morning Matt. Had to put in an extra phone just for Priscomb's hotline." Spender pointed to the phone and fresh wire. Arms crossed, he still had an officer's build, but all the weightlifting and exercise couldn't stop a receding hairline. "Priscomb didn't want to use our phone line . . . said we might miss a call if it's bunched in with the rest of our cases. But then, it's his money."

Spender stood, stretched, and reached for a coffee mug with the words PIG BOWL on the side. When he wasn't monitoring the phone lines, he was captain of the police football team.

"You here kinda early, aren't you?" Spender glanced at the clock. Seven-fifteen.

"You stayed the night?" I asked him.

"Yep. And if you're asking about the Redmond case, we didn't get one call."

"What about on your regular line?"

"We got seven calls, all for tips on other cases."

I twisted a plastic cup off the top of a stack next to the coffeemaker. "What's your take on the Redmond death?"

Spender untangled his arms, revealing a worn tattoo no longer readable from age. "I don't like to make assumptions. The badges in homicide don't, so I don't either. Besides, the only ones who make assumptions are reporters." A smile peeled across his face.

"We don't assume, we speculate." I took in another sip of the coffee. "I thought I'd stop by rather than call."

"I trust you." Spender stared at the silent phone.

He studied the arrangement of photographs. Most were black and white. Below the pictures were details of when and where a murder occurred and personal information about the victim.

"I stay up all night hoping to get one phone call. Just one. I've received my share of leads, don't get me wrong. I'd really like to get the tip to bust this Redmond case."

My pager thumped a steady beat until I checked the number and dialed the office.

"Mike? What's up?"

"Where are you Matt?"

"I'm in the pillbox checking on phone calls to Suspect Watch."

"There's some breaking news. We need you on this . . ."

"What's going on?"

"Stacy Gaines is dead."

Chapter Twenty-four

"You can't be sure about that!" I placed the cup down before I threw it at the wall.

"I'm sure, Matt."

"Who confirmed this? Who Mike?" My raised voice caused Spender to leave his post at the phones. He was standing next to me.

"What's up Matt?"

I ignored Spender. "Tell me, who confirmed this?"

"Matt, calm down. If you want me to get someone else on this—"

"No. I'll cover it. How can you be so sure it's her? Where's the scene?"

"The Everglades. Ike has the location. We just need you."

"I'm at the police station, should I check with anyone here?"

"They're all at the scene. I'm sorry to tell you this."

My Beemer just missed the rear panel of a slow moving Buick. The driver raised an arm, shook a fist at me, then he continued his ten-miles-under-the-speedlimit pace. It was still early and traffic wasn't a stranglehold just yet. My speedometer needle touched eighty-five until I stomped on the brake to avoid smashing into the back of a truck carrying stacks of empty wooden pallets. Stacy was a priority but I wanted Cat to hear from me before she saw something on a newscast. Her home was still two miles west of the inter-state. I adjusted my hands-free headset and speed-dialed Cat's number a second and third time but got no answer. Mike Brendon was my next call.

"Mike, where's the crime scene exactly?"

"Once you hit US Twenty-seven, go north. It's right next to the boat ramp."

"We have anything on the air yet?"

"Just a mention, but we didn't say the name."

"Did they say what happened?"

"Just that they found her. Listen Matt, you don't have to do this. We can put another reporter on this. Where are you now?"

"I'm close, but I'm still trying to get in touch with Cat. I have to reach her, but there's no answer."

"Tell you what, I'll send someone by to check on her. We need somebody in the Glades. Now. You sure you want to work this?"

I feel so much safer now.

Stacy's words came at me like shards, tearing away at the vision of security I pictured for her.

"Matt? You there?" Mike's voice kicked up in volume.

"I'm sorry. I'll swing by the station and hook up with Ike. But please, have someone check on Cat."

"It's done."

"Anything on the circumstances? Her car?"

"She had a rental car right? From what I can gather it's still outside her townhouse."

"Mike, where are we getting this information?"

"A video stringer is there, getting some videotape for us and taking notes. There's an active crime scene at the town-house and out west."

I passed the exit to Cat's neighborhood and kept going downtown. "Tell Ike I'll be at the station in ten minutes."

Chapter Twenty-five

I teamed up with Ike and we drove eighteen miles west of downtown Fort Lauderdale, to the Florida Everglades. The area was a vast wilderness of poisonous snakes and slow-moving water stretching to Florida's west coast.

Thoughts and images of Stacy flashed in my mind like so many movie clips. When we arrived, a tarp covered the body of Stacy Gaines while the investigators finished their work. She was several feet from the water in a public parking lot. A boat ramp of algae-stained concrete angled down into the black swirls of Glades water. Beyond the crime scene, the vast horizon of the Everglades stretched before me. I tried to call Cat several more times but the recorded voices of Shauna and Jason said leave a message.

I found Frank Walker near three unmarked police cars. "Any details yet?" My eyes stayed on the figure on the ground.

"A fisherman found her near the dock." I heard Walker's words but I couldn't perceive them as real. I just spoke to her hours before. Walker listened to my question and he moved toward the detectives as he answered me. "Let me find out what I can."

I walked the bank looking for something the detectives missed. Anything. A slight wind rippled the surface of the water, with the same deep hue of an alligator's back. A blue heron stood on the gray branches of a dead melaleuca tree.

To my right, a snake skin dried to a crispy touch on arcs of swaying sawgrass. I looked at the tarp and tried to replay the last several days and hours.

So safe.

Ike adjusted the camera on the tripod and pointed the lens at the tarp. "You okay?"

"Not really."

"Mike called a few minutes ago. There's no one at Cat's place. He wants to know if another reporter should come out. Says it's all right if you want to move off this story."

"I'll call him back. I can stay."

Two detectives raised the tarp while a crime scene technician moved in closer and photographed her. We couldn't see the body. Walker stepped around Ike and away from the microphone and kept his voice low. "All I can say is, it appears she was stabbed and not shot."

"Do the injuries look similar to Lane Redmond's?"

"Matt, you know I'm not a forensic type. I can't make that connection. I don't want folks thinking there is a serial killer loose until we get a finding from the ME and confer with homicide."

"I was with her last night. Along with Cat. They were roommates in college."

"What time were you there?"

"We left her townhouse at about nine. Cat had to drive me home and get back to her kids."

"Collins will want to speak to you and . . . what's her name, Cat?"

"That's her nickname. I've been trying to reach her."

Walker pulled out a pad, jotted something down and again walked off. He stepped past two men. One was wearing a long-billed fishing cap, faded blue jeans and T-shirt with a huge bass on the front. The other kept spitting into the tufts of grass which broke through cracks in the paved sections of the parking lot. He was taller, and kept his arms folded against his chest until he finally stepped away from the line of detectives and walked toward me. I tapped Ike on the shoulder and picked up the microphone.

"I'm Matt Bowens . . . Channel Fourteen. When you got here, what did you see?"

"We were getting ready to drop the boat in the water and there she was, right out in the middle of the parking lot. We stopped and checked her pulse but . . ."

"Was there anyone around? Any sign of a weapon?"

"We didn't see anything. Just the normal run of cars, a cab and a few trucks. And all that blood covering her chest. I mean a lot of blood. It's not the kind of thing you'd expect."

"Your name?"

"Walt. Walter Moore. We come here all the time, and you see all kinds of things out here, but not this."

"Could you see or hear a car in the area?" The question came from Sandra Capers. She eased her microphone next to mine. Moore blinked as if surprised by all the attention. "We didn't see anything. Just truckers rolling by."

"What was she wearing?" Capers moved in close to me, shoulder to shoulder.

"Just a . . . I guess you'd say she was well dressed. She was an attractive woman. It's a shame."

Detective Collins pulled at Moore's elbow and eased him away from the cameras. They kept going past us toward a metallic-green bass boat some twenty yards from us. Moore adjusted his fishing cap. He pulled a water bottle from his pants and took a swig. Collins led him far around our cameras on the way back to the array of detectives.

I could feel the stare of Capers. "I saw your story on Lane's husband. You were in the right place."

"Thanks, Matt."

Capers had to be close to six feet. She kept her hair tied back which meant the camera caught all of her smooth cheeks, brown eyes and attractive smile.

"I understand you knew the victim?" I didn't know how to take her question. Was she genuinely concerned or was she gauging me for information?

"I knew her. I regret I only knew her for a short time."

"She lived downtown?"

"Yes."

Walker approached the cameras at the same time the body removers arrived. "I can give you a statement, if you want." Walker jotted down a line on a pad of paper. The photographers aimed their cameras at Frank Walker. "At approximately six-thirty this morning, two fishermen found the body of a female. There are visible signs of trauma and at this time, we are canvassing the area looking for anyone who might have been involved in this homicide. We are asking the public, if anyone saw something this morning to please call police or the Suspect Watch hotline."

"Any link to Lane Redmond's death?" I asked.

"Not at this time. As you know that's an ongoing investigation and we can't speculate right now on how the two might be connected, if at all."

Capers brushed a line of hair flat against her forehead. "Can you give us a time line of her whereabouts in the past twenty-four hours?"

"From what we can figure, she was at home last night and beyond that, we can't guess what happened next. As you can imagine, we will be talking to her friends as well as the people she worked with."

Walker stepped back and away from the cameras. Over his shoulder, the removers finished wrapping up her body and they rolled the gurney to the van. The cameras tracked and recorded the movement.

A black limousine pulled up a few yards from the bass boat. The passenger-side rear door opened and William Jackels stepped into the sunshine. He buttoned his suit and adjusted the gray and black tie. A detective motioned to the removers and the gurney stopped at the rear doors of the van. Frank Walker escorted Jackels to the body. Jackels stood there while a detective gently removed the coroner's blanket from around her body. Jackels nodded and dropped his head toward the pavement. For a moment, her arms and chest were exposed to us. Jackels stood in silence while they wrapped her, and the gurney was eased into the van. The doors were slammed shut. The removers prepared to leave.

It sounded like a muffled voice at first. I could just hear it over the tires of the van which crunched up stalks of withered hyacinth and turned onto US 27.

Now the voice was a cry. Pure. Fiery, and full of anguish. I turned back to the limousine. The door was open and the cries grew in intensity until the wails became the dominant sound, rolling over the uneven pavement and echoing against the thick hammocks of Brazilian Pepper trees and wild cocoplum. Every detective, crime tech, reporter and photographer turned in the direction of the car. A woman emerged. In long strokes, she wiped down the tears from her face, then took in deep breaths at a spastic cadence. Uncontrolled and shaken. The usually powerful eyes were now weak. I could only think of protecting her, and getting her away to someplace . . .

. . . *safe.*

Her breathing was labored and uneven, and quivers shook the length of her body. Her face turned to a glare. I looked into the eyes of Cat Miller.

Chapter Twenty-six

My hug was firm and I took in the scent of Cat's body. Jackels stood off to one side, next to Detective Collins. A Channel 8 microphone was wrapped in the fingers of Sandra Capers. I could see the confusion in her face. Her photographer gripped the lens of the camera, attempting to focus the picture of a reporter hugging a grieving woman.

"I tried to call you." I turned Cat's body away from the camera.

"Mr. Jackels called me early this morning." She took a second to take in more air. "He said something happened to Stacy and he was sending his limousine over to pick me up."

"Did you call me?"

"Jackels said he called you." The tears welled again. "I just don't understand."

"Why did he bring you? You shouldn't be here."

"Don't blame him. I wanted to come."

"Did Jackels say what happened?"

"No. On the way he got a few phone calls. I guess they were detectives."

"When we left her townhouse, did you see anything that looked suspicious?"

"There was nothing. And after what happened with Stacy's car . . . I mean we all kept watch."

"You'll have to give Detective Collins a statement, so try to remember anything to help him."

"They want to see us." Jackels now stood near the door. The soft tissue under his eyes looked puffy from a lack of sleep. Ike started to step toward me, but I waved him off. I aimed my question at Jackels. "Did you talk to Stacy last night?"

"That's between me and the detectives, not the press." Jackels reached out for Cat's hand. "They're waiting."

Cat took his hand and they walked to the circle of detectives. Jackels kept a steady glance at the spot where they removed Stacy's body until he reached the group of investigators.

"I'm sorry I have to ask you Matt, but will your friend talk?" Another question from Sandra Capers.

"I don't think so."

"Could you ask her?"

"She's not talking. Stacy was a close friend and I don't think Cat's up to speaking to us right now."

I checked my watch: 10:45 A.M. A background noise of buzzing crackled through the Glades from a collection of bugs, and anything that might moved over the porous limestone. Cat and Jackels finished their talk with the detectives. Capers yelled a question to them as they neared the limo. They never looked up. The doors closed and the stretch of steel and wheels inched across the parking lot and into nearby traffic. Minutes after the car left, two live trucks turned into the lot. It was time to prepare for the noon newscast.

"You got a sec?" I knew Detective Hank Florzen from other investigations.

I put away the microphone and motioned to get Ike's attention. "I've got a few minutes," I told him.

Florzen led me back to where Detective Collins was turning off a cell phone. Ike trailed us by a few steps. "Your cameraman doesn't have to come."

"I want him there."

"He wasn't at the house. We just need a quick statement."

"It's either Ike or the Channel Fourteen attorney."

Florzen opened the door of a faded white sedan and pulled a towel from the passenger seat. He started on one side of his face and dragged the towel against the lines of sweat on his forehead. "Suit yourself, Bowens." Florzen placed the towel on his left shoulder, then whipped open a small note pad. Collins appeared uninterested, but he kept his body facing the trio of reporter, detective and photographer.

"What did you do at the apartment of Miss Gaines?"

"She wanted us to . . . I mean she wanted Cat and myself to look over the townhouse for security."

"Did you find any problems?"

"Not really. Her sliding glass doors needed some work but that was about all."

"Did she say she saw anyone?"

"No."

"Was she expecting anyone?"

"Not that she told us."

Florzen pulled the towel down from his shoulder for another swipe and slapped it back into place. "Any phone calls while you were there?"

"No."

"What time did you leave?"

"We left at about nine or so."

"Or so?"

"Nine. Cat had to get back to her kids."

"Did you return later?"

"What kind of question is that? Return and do what?" I felt myself edge closer into his space. It wasn't intentional, just an impulse move when anger controls your actions.

Ike pulled at my arm. "Matt."

"The questioning can stop right here," I said.

"Matt . . ." Now Ike was moving me back away from the detectives.

Florzen ignored the towel and removed a line of sweat with his hand. "Ease up Matt. There are no free passes here. You know that. Everyone gets a look by the police. And that means you."

"The look is over. Next time I'll check with the station

attorney before I say anything." I stepped away from Florzen to give me time to work off the boil until I looked into the lens of a Channel 8 photographer. I stopped for a moment then took up my spot near the bass boat. Capers aimed her microphone in my direction. "You can put it away Sandra. There's nothing to say right now."

"I hate to do this to you Matt, but what did you talk about with the police?"

I let the pause turn into moments, then a body of silence long enough for Sanders to finally lower the microphone. I waited until her photographer dropped his lens before I spoke. "I can't talk about this. Not yet. And definitely not here. There are too many things to nail down."

Capers rested the microphone against her side. "Nothing personal. I'm just trying to do my job."

Chapter Twenty-seven

I knocked. Cat's best friend in south Florida answered. GG Manor opened the front door to the sound of Jason erasing a smudge on a sheet of paper. Shauna sat on the couch flipping through a book.

GG's tight cornrows draped down her back. When she spoke, the muscles in her neck formed rigid lines with each word. "She's been resting." GG pointed me in the direction of the kitchen. "But it's time she ate something."

GG stepped toward Cat's bedroom and I took up a chair in front of a stack of sliced fruit. Muffled conversation drifted from the hallway until GG appeared first, leading Cat into the kitchen. Cat tracked baby steps into the room. Her hair needed to be combed, and her eyes were somber. She sat down as if unaccustomed to the ritual of eating.

"C'mon now. You know you've got to eat something." GG put the meal before Cat but she didn't stir.

I took my hand and interlaced my fingers with hers.

GG spoke to her. "C'mon Cat. The kids already ate. You got to put something in your stomach." GG stood as if she wouldn't move until Cat raised a fork.

Cat gripped my hand in a tight hold. "I don't want anything," she said. "Really."

I tried to connect with her eyes. "You need strength for Stacy and to find out what happened. The only way to do that is if you're strong."

"I need some coffee." Cat's body looked rigid.

"Okay." There was a tone of defeat in GG's voice.

I sensed the same downturn of emotions years before at the edge of my housing project. Someone shouted my name. Muzzle blast. A burning in my chest. The hot, sticky blood dripped from my hand. And then I was out. Oblivion. I don't know how long I stayed that way through the pain, until I heard the soft echoes from one edge of a crevice, holding on to life with death on the other side ready to pull me in. Faint images mixed with moments of clarity between the IV drip, a nurse checking my bandages, and a doctor explaining the wound to my mother. Tears from relatives lined my bed. My arms, legs, and body were all immobile. I sensed their anger for the person who pulled the trigger.

The same foreboding was on Cat's face, eager to find Stacy's murderer. I ran my hand across my chest. It's there, just to the right of my heart. A quarter-inch scar called a keloid.

Cat's eyes widened. "There was something missing." Her gaze stayed on the plate, never lifting her head.

"Missing?" I could feel fingers grip mine a bit tighter.

"I didn't think about it at first. I was so—"

Cat broke her fingers free and rubbed the weariness from her eyes. "Just for a moment there, I saw Stacy's hand. And it wasn't there, Matt."

"What?"

"The bracelet I gave her. It's the X's and O's bracelet. She never took it off. Never. It wasn't there."

"Maybe she left it in a hurry this one time?"

"No. I don't care what the situation, she never took that bracelet off. It matches mine." Cat raised up her left hand and showed me a gold bracelet. "She got me one on my birthday. The same kind. We always wore them. I only saw her for a few moments but I didn't see it on her arm."

GG adjusted the pot until it fit into the coffeemaker. "Did you tell the police?"

"I didn't think about it at the time. There was so much . . ."

She sagged back in the chair. I didn't want to see Cat in so much pain. There was a slight tremble in her voice.

"If she struggled, maybe it came off," Cat said. "But her arm didn't look like it had any marks, or scratches."

For a moment I pictured Lane Redmond's face again. And the crime techs who surrounded her before they covered the body. I turned to Cat. "When they found Lane, her left shoe was missing."

GG moved in slow motion and finished leveling two cups near the top. She offered, but I waved off the coffee. "Do you have a recent picture of Stacy?"

Cat eased forward. Her eyes flashed from the plate to GG lowering the cup to the table. "Give me a minute."

Cat pushed back from the table. Jason eased his head around the wall and peeked into the kitchen but he disappeared when Cat stood up. She stepped down the hallway. In a mother's voice, she warned Jason about finishing homework, and reminded Shauna a book had to be returned to the library. Then nothing. Cat returned admiring a small photograph. "This was taken three years ago, right after my divorce. GG and Stacy were part of my support team." Her lip turned up slightly.

She handed me the photograph. Cat and Stacy stood in front of the house. On Stacy's left arm, there was a shimmering gold bracelet.

Chapter Twenty-eight

I was in the office just minutes before my pager went off. The number looked familiar. Three rings later, the voice of agent Michael Ivory answered.

"Matt Bowens. You paged?"

"Did you ever run that interview we did?"

"Not yet. Why?"

"Good. It's outdated. We need to do another one. Hector Colon was spotted yesterday in Miami."

A poster-board blowup of Colon rested on an easel in a corner of the room. Ivory picked up the picture, easel and all, and put it in the center of the room. Above him on the wall, the words US ATTORNEY were in gold letters.

"Is this all right?" Ivory moved the picture over another inch. "This is a more recent photograph we just got in."

"It's fine." Ike extended the tripod legs and locked them into position.

"We don't have a lot of time," I began. "Unless this has a direct tie to the summit murders, I've got to move on."

"We're working weekends and some long hours because we want this guy. I want to get as much exposure as possible. The newspapers will be here in a few minutes." Ivory dropped back to his desk and pulled out a press release. There were two pages detailing the counterfeit charges,

Colon's history for violence, and where he was last seen in Miami.

"I know what you're thinking," Ivory said as he watched me go over the release. "I can't talk about the killings in Fort Lauderdale on camera. That's not Colon's style. When he kills, he leaves a mess."

He ran a hand over his hair. "I can tell you this. No one from law enforcement has contacted me about Colon in regard to the murders."

"What's next?" Ike finished photographing Colon's picture. I sat Ivory down for an interview. He started talking before Ike signaled the camera was on.

"Colon is always armed. He would not hesitate to use whatever means he had to avoid arrest."

Ten minutes later Ike packed the gear away. "I appreciate this." Ivory rarely smiled. "I just feel we are close. Real close."

"Any idea why he's still in the States?"

"None. I'm just glad he's close enough that we can grab him."

Chapter Twenty-nine

Wayne Poplin's words ended with the smack of gum being chewed. "Don't have a lot of time Matt. What's up?"

I caught Poplin on the telephone after two rings.

"Am I going down a bad path, or is there more to the connection between Colon and Senator Priscomb?"

"Before I answer that, what are you doing working on a Saturday?"

"Just thought I'd come in for a couple of hours and rake over the facts. Now, about Colon?"

"I don't know. What are you finding?" I heard Poplin tapping computer keys in the background. A few seconds passed before I answered him. I repeated as much as I dared without giving Poplin too much information from the feds. "Sounds like it's not very promising. Colon's a bad guy but I can't give you anything more. Miami assigned a reporter to track his movements."

"You'll have to excuse me," Poplin said. "I have four secretary candidates coming in Monday, I'm late on a project and I have a proposal to finish before then—"

"No problem."

"And there's still the big question."

"Question?"

"I'm sitting here not knowing if they're going to hire me to do the public relations end of the conference. I could use the gig." He sounded impatient. "And I have a deadline to bid my work to another project."

"You know a lot about the committee."

"I research my clients before I work for them."

I got off the phone with Poplin. Brendon was on the phone directing a Miami photographer to the western portion of the county to get video of the Florida Everglades. Dry conditions and a string of forty-plus days without rain, made the Glades ripe for brush fires. All four local stations were in the midst of Saturday morning broadcasts.

The newsroom was washed in January sunlight, and through the window the causeway was dotted with boats. I dialed Senator Priscomb's hotline number again.

"Yes."

"Is Senator Priscomb there?"

"He stepped away. He might be getting a bite. I'm not the regular person who answers this phone. Do you want to leave a message?" The voice sounded hurried.

I left my name and number. Before I took my eyes off the phone, it rang.

"Matt?"

"Yes."

"It's Spender. Suspect Watch. Is your newscast off?"

I looked up at the wall of television screens. Channel 14 was in a commercial. "Yeah, the newscast should end in a few minutes."

"Good. They waited."

"They?"

"The detectives. We've been working on a press release for the past hour. They want to release it this afternoon."

"Release what?" My voice must have kicked up because Mike Brendon turned and Ike stopped his walk to the door.

"I can't say what's in the release but they wanted to get the wording just right."

"C'mon Spender. You wouldn't be calling unless it was something major. What's going on?"

"I don't want to steal their thunder. I don't think they'll mind if I told you about the press release. Just be there."

"It always helps if we get some sense of what it's about. But trust me, we'll be there."

"Have you been in touch with Senator Priscomb?"

"I tried to call him but I was told he was out."

"Priscomb will be there."

"Where?"

"The release will tell you all about it. They told me it was okay if I called, but you should get a fax any minute now from the PIO. What's his name?"

"Frank Walker."

"That's right, Walker."

Brendon stood up from his desk.

"Spender, you're using up the dime. What do we have?"

"They're going to name a suspect."

Chapter Thirty

Walker called as the fax came through the machine. I snatched the paper and grabbed the telephone.

"We'll make our announcement at 2 P.M." Walker began. "We'll have Detective Collins there along with a portion of the homicide unit and Senator Priscomb will be there as well."

"Can you say—"

"You'll have to come to the news conference. When Spender told me he was going to give you a call, I told him to contact everyone. We don't play favorites here."

"If you give me some idea of who—"

"Don't even go there." There was a finality in Walker's tone. "Two P.M. You'll get everything you need."

His last word was followed by dial tone. Mike looked over my shoulder to read the release. "Let's plan on taking this announcement live. I'll give engineering a call and get them started to set up the room. Two microphones. You and the podium. Later, you can do a live hit for the Six. You can concentrate on the suspect. All the details. Lankin will be there to do reaction."

"No problem."

I picked up the phone and dialed Cat's number at work. She wasn't able to come talk, so I left a message to make sure she was in front of a television at 2 P.M.

* * *

Four tripods lined the conference room in the pillbox. On the podium, a mass of microphones was bunched together. Black cables stretched from the podium to cameras and out the door to other hookups. The parking lot was lined with live trucks and satellite units. Photographers checked for lighting. Ike aimed his camera toward the podium. Frank Walker stood in front of the arrangement of microphones. He looked around the room. "When we start, I will make a few comments, then Detective Collins will make a statement. They will be out in a few minutes."

Again I checked my watch: 1:59 P.M. We were set to broadcast live in one minute. Frank Walker panned the room, left to right. A voice was in my earpiece again, giving me a countdown. "We're coming to you in thirty seconds Matt." Walker coughed a couple of times to clear his throat.

"Fifteen seconds, Matt." There would be one last cue.

Only the hum of the overhead fluorescent lights could be heard in the room.

"Five seconds."

Behind Walker, Detective Collins stood at military at-ease. Senator Priscomb was on his right. A few yards away, Spender leaned against the wall with his arms crossed. In my ear, I heard the jingle music and the announcer say this was a special report. I started talking, but I could hear the words of other reporters standing just inches from me.

"Good afternoon, this is Matt Bowens at the headquarters of Fort Lauderdale-Metro Police. We are about to hear the latest on the investigation into the deaths of two members of a summit conference team. Lane Redmond was found murdered four days ago, and yesterday, the body of Stacy Gaines was found in the Everglades. Police are now saying they might have a suspect. For that, we turn to police spokesman Frank Walker."

Walker waited until the last reporter finished an introduction. "Thank you. For the past several days our detectives have been working around the clock to find the leads to direct us toward a person or persons. I want Detective Collins to give you an idea of where we stand in this case."

Walker stepped back and Collins moved in front of the gathering of microphones.

"I want to say first of all that we are not calling this person a suspect. This is someone that we very much would like to speak with."

Collins turned to Spender. A large picture was turned to the wall. Spender turned it around and carried the huge photograph and an easel to the podium. He placed the picture to the right of Collins. Every camera in the room followed the actions of Spender.

"This is the man we want to speak to. His name is Gregory Wilding." Collins paused for a moment. Reporters jotted notes in their pads.

"Without getting too much into details, enough evidence has been gathered for us to ask the public for help in finding Mr. Wilding, so that we may question him about the events in the past several days. He is a convicted stalker who spent twenty-nine months in jail, and was released last June to a halfway house. At the very least, he has violated the court's guidelines to contact his probation officer. We showed photographs and we're getting confirmation that he was seen in the area of where Lane Redmond lived. If anyone has seen Mr. Wilding, we would urge that you contact the homicide unit or call Suspect Watch."

When Collins paused again, I yelled a question. "You say you have evidence to link Mr. Wilding. What evidence?"

Collins looked at Spender and Walker before he answered. "Our detectives have gathered evidence from the crime scenes to suggest that Mr. Wilding was there. Again, we would very much like to speak to him."

"What evidence? Fingerprints?"

"We have DNA evidence to show Mr. Wilding was at those crime scenes."

To my right Sandra Capers asked the next question. "DNA can take days. You've been able to detect a DNA connection that quickly?"

"I'm not the expert on this," Collins started. "I just know that we have tests, or rather there are tests available to give us a quick read on a DNA result. I don't have to tell you the value of DNA testing. A few years ago, DNA results meant one man was freed from a Florida prison after twenty years behind bars. It's now mandated that most Florida inmates give DNA samples. And the legislature has created a network for inmates to appeal on the basis of DNA. But in this case, we feel confident on the reasons why we want to speak to Mr. Wilding."

Another question from my left. "If you knew Wilding was involved in the first homicide, why did you wait so long to make this announcement?"

Collins waited a moment before answering. "Let me say that we have been actively looking for this person and tracking down dozens of leads. We just recently got a DNA match and when we got a second match to Mr. Wilding, we thought we should go public."

I waited for another moment to speak. "Can we speak to Senator Priscomb? We'd like to get his reaction."

Collins waited until Priscomb reached the microphones before he moved back. "There isn't that much to say right now. The investigation is still at an early, pivotal stage. We are all hoping for some closure and an arrest. I just want to applaud the work of the police to get us to this point."

"One more question." Walker's voice boomed from behind Priscomb.

Sandra Capers got the last word. "Do you have any reason to believe he's still in the area?"

"We checked all the places he has been known to frequent. Mr. Wilding has worked in restaurants, and odd jobs. We just think he's here."

I spoke over the live video of the photograph of Wilding. In my television monitor, I could see a tight close-up of him. We stayed on that photograph while I gave my sign-off. I waited for Miami in my ear.

"You're clear Matt. Thanks."

The crews moved in closer for a better video shot of Wilding. Ike made Walker place the picture in a better location. Senator Priscomb almost made it out the door.

"Senator, did a tip come in on your hotline number?"

"No. Just good police work." He kept edging toward the door. "Someone will continue to sit in on the hotline, but we are leaving this afternoon."

"Leaving?"

"Yes. I've got a driver to take us up tonight. We're moving Lane's remains up to Tallahassee where we can have a funeral service."

"At some point will you return? I know how you want to see this through."

"I don't know if my wife can go through the strain. It's been tough on everyone. We're thinking about taking a trip out of the country. Thanks for your help."

He walked hunched over so the silver and black tips of his long hair touched the top of his suit. In the conference room, Walker was passing out a new press release. It listed Wilding's last known two addresses, his rap sheet, age, height, and known habits. The release did not call him a suspect. And Collins was already gone.

Ike lifted his face from the camera eyepiece.

"Anytime the police say they want to talk to someone, that person is a suspect. I don't care what they say."

I pulled out my cell phone to call Brendon. He picked up after two rings.

"It looked good Matt. So what do we do this afternoon?"

"If you want to change things, I can do the nuts and bolts. But I'd like to get over to Wilding's last address before the horde does. I can give the interview with Senator Priscomb to Lankin for his sidebar piece. Do we need a case number on that stalking conviction to find the victim?"

"Walker says he will fax some information over," Brendon said.

"If she wasn't harmed, we need some clue as to why Wilding graduated to murder."

"I'll send Lankin by Wilding's old neighborhood, the second address. Check back in an hour. We're thinking about having you go live from the police hotline phone bank."

"That sounds fine."

Detective Collins came back into the room. "Matt, I don't have much time."

He put both hands on his back and gave a sigh. "This isn't the way we wanted to do this." He kept looking at Wilding's photograph.

"How is your friend holding up? What's her name? Cat?"

"Not too well. They were very close. I need to ask you . . . did you pick up anything missing from Stacy's body?"

"Like?"

"Cat says she always wore a bracelet. One she gave Stacy in college. But she didn't see it."

"I'll make a note of it. Did she think of anything else?"

"That was it."

"If she does, can you make sure she calls me?" Collins reached for a card from his pocket.

"Now . . . that's for her, not you."

"Is there any reason to believe this is the guy who went at me?" Thoughts about the kicks made me run my hand down my side.

"That's still out there. We just don't know. He could have been trailing Stacy. Your description of his height and weight matches, but you never got a good look at his face."

"What will we find at Wilding's address?"

"Not much. We just hope if his picture gets out there, we'll get a phone call."

Lankin approached. Collins dropped back amid the room of people rolling up cables, and packing away television lights.

"Mike told me what you're looking for. I'm headed to the second address now." Lankin turned from me to the picture of Wilding. "If you can think of another angle, let me know."

Chapter Thirty-one

I arrived at the address of the first house on the list just as Sandra Capers was getting out of her car. The one-story stucco home had to be at least forty years old. A number of plants in clay pots rested on bricks to the right of the door. The end of each plant leaf was tipped in dead brown. Rain droplets from past storms had dried to dusty patterns on the windows. Capers slipped on a pair of running shoes, and left the pumps in the car. A faded newspaper served as a door-mat. I knocked. The door felt fragile.

"Go away!" The muffled voice came from somewhere inside.

"We just want to ask you a question or two, that's all." Capers leaned in and talked to the doorjamb. We both gave our names and waited.

"I said go away." The voice was stronger now, as if someone moved closer to the door. I knocked again.

"Go ask the police your questions!" Now it sounded like the voice was just on the other side of the door. "The man's not guilty."

I glanced back at Ike. His camera was up on his shoulder, recording every second. "We just want to hear that from you."

Silence. We waited perhaps ten minutes.

"It's four-forty." The photographer who was working with Capers offered the time check. It meant a six o'clock news deadline was approaching. We both left and checked other

129

houses on the block to see if someone heard of Wilding. No answer. Another ten minutes wasted. Capers knocked again at the first address, waited, then stepped away. She probably figured the voice behind the door didn't want to talk, and there were other matters to check elsewhere. Ike eased the camera back from his shoulder. Capers nodded her photographer back to the car. The reasons a reporter decided to leave a scene can vary. She was probably concerned about her deadline, and the fact we were getting zero information. It was down to the game of who would blink first. Sandra Capers flashed a combatant's smile. Then she left. It was her decision to go. Her car rolled out into the street and turned toward the intersection. Ike dumped gear in the van. We were also about to leave. My beeper thumped a mild vibration.

"My battery is getting low." The readout on my pager said Mike Brendon was trying to reach me. I reached for my cell phone. Two rings and Mike answered. His voice came at me in pieces of sentences. Garbled and full of static.

"I can't hear you," I shouted into the phone.

". . . you need to know . . ." They were the only words I could make out from Mike. I jammed the phone back in my pocket.

"I need to get to a spot where I can call Mike." Ike wasn't paying attention to me. His gaze was fixed on the front of the house. I looked in the direction of his stare.

The door was open.

I felt a sudden gust. A south Florida wind tapped at the three palm trees in the yard. A gathering of storm clouds teased the possibility of rain. The air smelled moist like trapped layers in a fog. I walked up the sidewalk, passed a rusty spade, a few empty beer cans, and the tall uncut grass.

When I reached the opened door, it creaked in the breeze. There was no air-conditioning. I pushed the door open just a bit and the house released its breath of musty air and dry heat. In one corner, there were piles of clothing. Sweaters, torn jeans, and wrinkled T-shirts rested against a milk crate. On top of the crate, I saw my reflection in the black screen of a small television.

"Hello?" My voice didn't carry well.

"You say you wanted to know why I think he didn't do this." I couldn't locate the voice. "I'd say come on in but you're already in."

I pushed the door open wider, but I bumped into something. Behind the door, there was a shopping cart, full of empty plastic bags. I didn't hear him step into the room. A gray stubble covered his chin and neck. He was bald except for a few white strands. His pants were too tight and his shirt had a large tear on the pocket. Every window in the place was closed and the scent of an unflushed toilet drifted from the bathroom. His slate-gray eyes started at my shiny shoes, then up to my silk tie.

"My name is Matt—"

"I know who you are. Seen you on TV. All the time. All the time. Channel Eight, isn't it?"

"Channel Fourteen."

"That's right, Fourteen."

"I just wanted to talk to you about—"

"Greg?"

"Yes. Greg Wilding. And your name?"

"My name isn't important right now. If you push it, you can just go back out that door." He raised a finger toward the outside.

"It's okay. No name. What can you tell me about him?"

He started to answer but stopped when Ike entered the room. Ike surveyed the inside. His expression looked like he wanted to leave.

"This is Ike. We're working together to find out about Wilding. And to hear what you have to say about these allegations."

"The what?"

"All the things the police are saying." I took the microphone from Ike's hand. "Any idea where Greg Wilding is now?"

Seconds passed while he studied Ike. He stared at the microphone, then back up to the camera before answering.

"I last saw him three weeks ago. He was going to the store

or something, and he never came back. He never left a word or anything."

"The police say he might be linked to two murders. The victims were killed within days of each other."

"I know what the police say, but I don't know if Greg has it in him to do that. He never gave me that notion. I saw what the police said. Made me miss my sports. They said some terrible things. Some terrible things."

"Did he stay here long?"

"Off and on about six months."

"Did he work? Have a job somewhere?"

"Greg got his money some kind of way. He had some beat-around jobs. You know, nothing special. Just something for the PO."

"PO?"

"His probation officer. Had to have a job to stay out of trouble." He dropped his hand inside his pants to reshuffle the shirt inside the tight fit. "I'm telling you everything I told the police."

I stopped the questions. "Is is okay if we see his room?"

"Sure, the police already been in there. They took all kinds of stuff?"

"Like?"

"Some of his clothing, and a piece of the rug. Cut it clean down to the tile. I need to rent this room out, that's how I make my money. But it looks so bad in there."

He led me down a narrow hallway and a second bedroom. A black layer of fingerprint powder covered the bathroom countertop, the dresser and areas around the door. The clean sections on the countertop indicated where the crime techs lifted fingerprints with tape. The same long rectangular clean spots were on the dresser and door. Plastic blinds covered the windows.

"How long were the police in here?"

"All day yesterday. Made me leave until they were done."

I kept thinking about Sandra Capers. She left just moments before the door opened. I checked the rest of the room. A bookcase rested between two closed windows.

"Don't believe in air-conditioning?" I asked.

The crop of stubble covering his chin bunched up. "Can't afford it."

"What about opening the windows?"

"Tried that. I don't have much, but I had three burglaries in two weeks. Thieves took my television. New TV cost me twenty bucks at the thrift shop. Now I keep everything closed up, locked up."

The ceiling fan above me provided the only movement of air. Each blade had a thick coating of dust. "You know there are programs out there to get you air-conditioning if you can't afford it."

"Where?"

"Tell you what, I'll get you the information."

"Thank you." He opened drawers to show me Greg's clothes were still packed away. A drawer next to the bed was still open. It was lined with empty and half-filled bottles of Jack Daniels and vodka.

"Greg likes a taste every now and then." He eased the drawer back into the closed position. The bottles rattled with the push.

"Greg comes here to crash, doesn't he?"

"Not all the time. Just when he's—"

"Drunk?"

He ran his fingers against the prickly stubble. "I suppose so. He came here to . . . rest."

"By rest, you mean drink?"

"A lot. If his PO found out, he might be in trouble. He could violate his probation just for sipping a taste."

"Does he do things when he's drunk?"

Hundreds of interviews taught me to look for signs of lying. A look away. A blink. Hesitation. Even a change in mid-sentence pushed the needle on my lie-meter. I searched the face. He stared directly at me. No wavering.

"He sleeps. That's about it. Once I came home and found him leaned up against the front door. Couldn't even wake him up . . . had mosquito bites all over him."

"How often does he come here?"

"I already told you. The deal is . . . he comes here to rest up. He pays me in full ahead of time in cash and I keep this room for him so he can sleep it off."

Ike rested the camera back on his shoulder. "I shot everything twice. But there's not much to shoot here."

"Greg blacks out sometimes," the man began. "The liquor does it."

I stepped from the heat of the house and into the cool air just outside the door. A storm breeze whipped the palm trees, and lightning ripped a white streak down the gut of a cloud.

"We've got just enough time to make it," Ike said, speeding up his pace. Another lightning bolt scratched a jagged line in the sky. A few seconds later, the deep tones of thunder sounded like explosions. Ike slammed the van door closed and we prepared to leave. Fingers tapped at my window and I hit the down button on the van door.

"I'll give you my name." He started talking before the window stopped moving. "It's Olton Banyan. But everyone calls me O." I could hear the first few drops of rain hitting hard surfaces and anything metal.

"Okay, O." I wrote his name in my pad. "I need a favor."

A white flash lit up the yard, washing Olton's face in an eerie brilliance. "If Greg comes back, can you give me a call?" I extended my business card. A single rain drop hit it just as he took the card.

"Funny. The cops said the same thing."

We heard more thunder and Olton backed away from the van, examining the business card.

Ike reached for the dashboard, and wiper blades dragged across the windshield. The sky turned to gray stew and the thunder sounded distant. I weighed the options of how to start my story. By the time I reached the live truck one single moment in the day kept kicking at me. Why was Senator Priscomb so eager to leave when the killer might be arrested at any time?

Chapter Thirty-two

W hen I reached the live truck, Ron Lankin was waiting for me. The reporter sat in the truck going over some notes. The rain slowed and the ground water simmered with the afternoon sun. Ike pulled the videotapes from the protection of his raincoat and slid one of them into the editing machine in the truck. Video of Greg's room came up on the monitor.

"What a dump." Lankin stopped flipping the pages of his pad.

"That's Greg's room," I told him. The room looked like the final stop of a desperate man. "The owner gave us a tour."

"Was Capers there?"

"She left."

A smile moved across Lankin's face. "Exclusive?"

I opened my pad. "I know we're splitting up the story, but did you get anything on the fax?"

Lankin lowered his eyes from the television monitor, back down to his notes. "According to the fax, the case file shows that Wilding pleaded no contest to an open count of stalking. In lieu of jail time, he was given three years probation."

He paused while he checked the next few pages. "The judge ordered him to counseling, with another order that he wasn't supposed to drink alcohol or go near the victim. When police found him, he had wrapped his Mercedes around a—"

"Mercedes?"

"Yeah. According to the documents, it was an SL Four hundred."

"Not bad."

I looked up at the video of the ripped carpet and the ceiling fan. "This guy crashes at night in this dust bowl of a room and he's driving around in an expensive car?"

"The car was totaled," he continued. "He wrapped it around a utility pole. And he lost his license for a year."

"When did the accident happen?" I wrote down as much as Lankin gave me.

"Fourteen months after his sentence."

"Did they get him for DUI?"

"Well, he passed up the breath test, so it's just about automatic. The license is lost for a time."

"But there was nothing in the judge's order about not driving after the sentence was up?"

"No."

"They released Wilding before someone checked the details on the probation order. If they saw the alcohol notation, he'd still be behind bars."

"I can see why he disappeared." Lankin closed his pad.

"Not to mention two murders." I pointed to the monitor. "I keep thinking about the money. It's not much but he paid his rent in cash. Was he still working?"

"He once sold homes for Cromin Realty. But they haven't seen him in a long time."

"What do you have on the stalking victim?" I asked.

He started going through his notes again. "She was someone he met at work. They went out once and when he couldn't convince her to go on a second date, he started showing up. Everywhere."

Ike glanced at his watch.

"We'll start in a few . . ." I said. Lankin appeared to be finished. "Did they fax a PC?"

Lankin reached down by his side and handed me a thin folder. Inside, the top page was marked Probable Cause Affidavit.

"It's six pages." Lankin took off his sport coat and rested

it on the back of the driver's seat. The shoulders of the coat were rain-soaked to a dark blue. The front page listed Wilding's name next to the word defendant. The permanent address listed for Wilding was different than the ramshackle dive he used for drunken binges.

"You go by there?" I asked.

Lankin closed up his writing pad. "It's a condo. Closed up tight. It would be easier getting a raise than getting into that place. But no, he wasn't there."

"You wait for someone to come out?" I asked.

"Took almost forty minutes before a couple of people confirmed Wilding hasn't been seen in weeks. They don't think he lives there anymore."

Below Wilding's address, age, and sex, were the charges in the stalking case. On the next line, the stalking victim's name was Anita Fulton. Below her name was a narrative from the detective. He wrote short sentences about Wilding.

Waiting outside victim's house. Defendant became more aggressive each time he was warned to stay away. Police units called on four occasions. Defendant showed up at the grocery store and followed victim to her car. Afraid he might be armed. On October 16th, 8:45 p.m., Defendant broke into victim's home and tried to speak to her. Police called.

I tapped the paperwork and flashed through dark thoughts about what happened to Stacy. Wilding could have been the one at the hotel room, trying to jimmy the door. He probably didn't want to break in, just let her know he was somewhere out there lurking. Stalking. It wouldn't be hard to tail Stacy to Cat's driveway, leaving himself plenty of time to work on the lock to her car. And Wilding was the right height and weight for the man who tried to pile-drive his boots into my side. The covering on his face left me with only a shadowy glimpse of my attacker.

I placed the folder on the dashboard. "The question is, what would make him move to another level and commit murder?" Another question kept bothering me. "There's a part missing," I started. "In all this paperwork, we still don't have a clear connection between Wilding to Lane and Stacy, except . . ."

"The MO." Lankin finished my sentence. "Stalking is Mr. Wilding's favorite activity and maybe our victims got his attention?"

I moved out of the way so Lankin could edit his story. At exactly 5 P.M., we both stood in front of the cameras and gave south Florida the best information we had.

To the west in the Everglades, a curving line of black smoke stretched from a narrow base to a wide plume against a mixed sky. Rain storms formed just to the north of me and I saw clear open stretches of blue to the south. Lightning probably caused the brush fires in the Glades.

"We just made it before the wet stuff hit." Ike pointed toward the rolls of gray clouds.

Lankin stepped around a puddle. "I found out the judge was notified about the drunk driving charge and a hearing was set for last Thursday about his probation. Wilding was a no-show because they couldn't locate him to serve the paperwork." He unloosened his tie and slid the reporter pad into his suit pocket.

"You working this story tonight?" Lankin asked.

"No one asked yet."

"You know Brendon. Since you worked this from the beginning, he might not want to give it to the night guys."

"I have no problem with that."

Ike slammed the van door. "I never turn down overtime."

"I'll call Mike and let him know I'll work the story. But I have a phone call and one stop to make first."

Chapter Thirty-three

"**I**'ve been watching your stuff on the news." Wayne Poplin eased a closet door shut, then sat in front of a computer.

"I don't have long," I told him. "I just have a favor. In your time during PR work, did you ever represent Cromin Realty?"

"Why? Is there some connection to something?" It was perhaps the first time I didn't see Poplin working a cheek of gum.

"Old records tell us Greg Wilding worked for Cromin, and I'm just wondering if you or anyone did any ads for them. I mean, did they only do homes, commercial property, or what?"

Poplin let his fingers move over the computer keyboard. "Before I started my own firm, we did a lot of work with realty agencies, but I can't remember if we did any jobs for Cromin. Our thing was new condominium projects."

"Well, before I knock on the door of Cromin Realty I want a better picture of everything they've done in south Florida. If you run across anything, please let me know."

"I'll do what I can," he said.

Jason jumped into a huge box of plastic balls, immersing his head and body in the multicolored spheres. A loud crunching noise caused heads to turn in the fast food restaurant. I could only track Jason by the movement of balls until he came up for air. Shauna bit into a french fry. She kept her left leg moving rapidly up and down, tapping her foot to the beat of a child working off boundless energy. Her burger was half-eaten. Jason's child box meal was on the table, unopened.

"Jason, come eat!" Cat waited for a response, but Jason only stood up and crashed head first into the pile of plastic. I looked through the window into the adult section of the restaurant. Ike pushed another burger into his mouth. All of us in this business ate too fast. My stare came back to Cat's downturned eyes.

"We had to get out of the house." Cat dipped a french fry into a small paper cup filled with ketchup. "I'm trying to get my mind off things. The police have anything new?"

"I thought you wanted to stay away from this?"

"I can't."

"There's really nothing since the news conference. But we're checking on a few things." I bit into my burger, half hoping Cat would change the topic. Jason rose from the depths of the playpen long enough to get a fix on our table, then he dropped back into the mounds of yellow, blue and orange balls.

"The last night we spoke to her, do you remember any hint of something wrong?" I bunched up an empty burger wrapper into a tight wad.

"She never mentioned a phone call, or a visitor. I've been thinking about it all day," Cat said.

"If she had a problem, wouldn't she try to call you?"

Shauna stopped eating and Cat gathered up her cup.

"Go play honey." Shauna skipped to the edge of the plastic ball pen, and stopped. She turned away from Jason and opted to climb inside the grid of tubular tunnels above us. Jason watched Shauna get on her knees and travel the interconnected pathways.

"Jason!" Cat yelled. Again he ignored the plea and joined Shauna in the tubes. "His food is going to get cold." Cat pulled in his meal next to her. The clear, bright eyes were serious, but turned moist. "Stacy would have called me." Her words had a depressed tone.

Cat worked back a tear.

"The police say there were no signs of forced entry," I began. "If it's the same person, both Stacy and Lane would know him well enough to let him in."

"Him? You mean, Wilding?"

"Cat, there's nothing to indicate Greg Wilding knew either of them—"

"It's Wilding! Why are you saying this? It's Wilding." Two women with toddlers glanced up from their burgers. Cat lowered her voice. "He's the one. The police even said they had DNA. They've got to find him."

I locked on her eyes. "You get what I mean? For Lane and Stacy to open that door, it would take a familiar face. Like Lane's father, or her ex-husband."

The simmer in Cat's voice was now a raging boil. "Stop going down this road, Matt. The police are convinced this is the suspect."

"There's nothing in Wilding's background to suggest he even *knew* them."

"There's just one thing *I* know. He is a vicious animal, a stalker and a killer. And if I have to, I'll find him myself." She raised her head to the network of green tubes. "Jason, Shauna come down here now!" Within seconds, they both emerged. First Shauna, then Jason.

"We're leaving Matt." Cat waved a finger at me. "The only thing I want to hear is that they captured this man. And then I want to face him myself. For Stacy and for Lane." Her words were as rigid as the tight lines in her face. "And you better give up on giving this guy a break."

And then she was gone. There was a stillness in the room. A shift in our relationship. I could feel it as strong as the change before an afternoon storm.

Chapter Thirty-four

Anita Fulton's address was the last house on Surf Drive, close to the beach line. I glanced over my notes, checking facts about her stalking encounters with Greg Wilding. About twenty minutes of daylight remained. No one was home when Lankin knocked hours before. I rapped at the door. No answer. Ike never raised the camera to his shoulder.

"There's nobody home. It's a dead end, Matt. Let's go."

I surveyed the area around the house. There were sand-covered sidewalks. The trunks of the palm trees were faded gray and looked like stone. A lone figure walked along the beach. The house probably offered little protection from noises. I imagined Wilding breaking in through a back door.

The woman on the beach came closer. "Let me just ask her a question and we're off."

Ike drew back to the van. I trudged in her direction. My shoes felt like weights. She stopped at a spot near the water and dug her toes in the wet sand. She did not move as I approached.

"Do you know if a person named Anita Fulton lives at that house?"

"I do." The woman barely looked at me before turning her attention to the surf which swirled around her feet. I had a brief look at her eyes. Green in color.

"What do you want with her?"

"I just wanted to ask her a question."

"Are you with the police?" The rain was gone and the sun dipped low, branding an outline of palm trees and apartment buildings in the red glow. She angled her head west to take it in.

"No. I'm Matt Bowens. I work for Channel Fourteen, and I'm looking for Anita Fulton. Do you know her?"

"Do you like sea shells?" Her question threw me a bit.

"Yes, but you'll find most of them on Florida's west coast."

"Very good." She dropped down into a squat and pressed her hands into the coarse granules. "Every now and then you can still find a good one on this side of the coast."

She turned back from the sunset and I tracked her stare to watch a column of cobalt waves break and stretch across the sand, delivering a thick foam on the shore. She rubbed the sand from her hands.

"Over there you can get all kinds of shells. Tulip conch, Bay scallop, and cockle shells. Here, you just have to keep looking."

She had an angular face, colorless lips pulled tight against the teeth, and her dark hair was combed by the wind. Her body was always turned just enough to make it difficult to see her eyes. She wiggled a big toe, digging her foot down in the sep-arating sand until it was past her ankles, but a rush of water washed over her feet to reveal a heart-shaped tattoo on the side of her calf. My shoes were getting wet and I stepped back.

"You're Anita Fulton, aren't you?"

She didn't answer me and started a slow pace toward the house. "What if I am? Then what?"

"I just wanted to talk to you. Just for a moment about Greg Wilding."

She stopped. Her eyes were fixed on me. Firm and direct.

"I hope they catch him." Her pace started again. Quick, controlled steps in the surf. She raised an arm in the direc-tion of an apartment complex. "I spent the entire day at a friend's house, trying to avoid all the reporters."

As she walked, a purse banged against her side. On the beach it looked oddly out of place.

"The police are looking for him," I said. The deep sand slowed my steps. "Your insight can help us know more about him—"

She cut me off. "When I woke up that night, Greg was right in my face. I can still smell that breath of warm beer."

We paused at the edge of her property. "I feel for what happened to those women, I really do. I mean the senator lost his daughter. Maybe if I talk . . ." She stepped up on the concrete. "After Greg confronted me in the middle of the night, I didn't see any cameras out here. There wasn't this mass of concern."

"Can I talk to you about it?"

She studied my face for several seconds, probably considering my question. Fulton turned and I watched her leave a trail of wet footprints on the concrete until she reached for her door. "C'mon inside."

I let Ike step inside the home first. He pointed to a couch and set up his camera gear. I studied the room. A line of conch shells were on a shelf over the door to the kitchen. Photographs of her with a man rested on a table near the couch. She lined herself up in front of Ike's camera and sat down. The purse stayed snug against her body.

She watched me admiring the picture. "That's my fiancé. I won't be Fulton anymore. In just three months, it will be Mrs. Craiger."

Ike put a microphone on her as she picked up the photograph, and studied the picture. "He'll be here after he gets off work."

Ike stepped behind the camera and gave me a nod. The camera was recording.

"What can you tell me about Gregory Wilding?"

She released a deep breath. "I thought he was nice at first. A great smile, and he had a pleasant voice on the phone. I didn't think he'd turn into a . . ." She paused. "I'm sorry. I didn't mean to stop."

"It's okay. You can keep going. You met him at work?"

"Yes. I just finished getting my real estate license and

Greg was the first one to greet me when I walked into the office at Cromin Realty. Three days later he asked me out."

"And did you go?"

"Not at first. I was concentrating so much on showing my first few homes, I was too busy. It was a month before he asked again."

"And what happened?"

"He took me to this quiet restaurant. Then he suggested we come back here. I hesitated, but he was so insistent. In a nice way."

She started to fumble with her hands. During my next question, Ike angled the camera toward her overlapping fingers, then back up to her face.

"And when you got home?"

"He wanted to come in, but I made him leave."

"He left?"

"He didn't want to at first, but he finally went home."

"Was there a second date?"

"The second date, I let him inside for a few minutes. That was our last date. And then it all started to happen."

"What happened?"

"He just changed. I mean, he kept leaving messages for me on the phone. Greg would say strange things. He would believe I was wearing a certain color dress, just for him. And he kept staring at me at work. I made up all kinds of excuses to leave the room. He tried to date, but I wasn't interested. That only made him increase the messages."

"Did you approach management about it?"

"Not for a long time. I was new, and Greg was near the top in sales. I tried to get more involved in my work and not think about him. Soon, my home sales were coming easier, and I was moving up. The manager liked the number of my close-outs. Greg's sales started to go down. Then one day . . ."

She stopped and rested a hand on top of the purse. "I was showing a home just off US One. When I show a vacant home, I always get there long before the buyer to make sure it's clean. Greg was standing there in the kitchen, waiting for me. I can't tell you how scared I was. He tried to approach me, but I ran out of there."

"And your boss?"

"I had to tell him. He understood. Greg was called into the office and put on suspension for a week. Without pay. It was easy enough for him to get the key and make a copy. While he was suspended, I noticed him following me to my appointments. That was the first time I called the police."

"Any charges?"

"Not then. The police talked to him and for awhile I thought everything was okay. Until he broke in my house."

"You were alone that night?"

"Yes. I was especially tired and went to bed early. At first I didn't hear anything. But the broken glass woke me up. The next thing I know, Greg had his hands on my mouth telling me not to scream. I tried to get up but he kept me pinned down. He kept telling me he just wanted a date. He would repeat it over and over. A date, he kept saying. I wanted to yell, but instead I calmed him down. It took every ounce of control in me, but I made him think I was okay with him breaking in."

Anger burned into her eyes. The purse was moved from her side to her lap. "Turn off the camera."

"I just have a few more—"

"Please turn off the camera."

I nodded to Ike and he eased back from the tripod. Anita's body shook. I watched her hug the purse tight against her chest.

"When did you get it?" I asked.

"Get what?"

"The gun?"

"Is the camera off?"

"It's off."

She pulled back the folds of the purse. It appeared to be a nine millimeter with pearl handles.

"Right after the break-in I got a concealed weapons permit. I don't want the world to know I'm carrying it. You understand, don't you?"

"I won't mention the weapon. I only have a few more questions." I paused for a response. She glanced down at the gun, finally closing up her purse and sliding it back down to her side and nodded. I signaled to Ike to continue. The camera was again recording.

"You say you calmed him down?" I asked.

Anita drew in a breath and held it for several seconds before answering. "I talked to him real nice. Soon, I gained his confidence. He kept talking about the one date we had. But I knew he had a drinking problem and I could tell he had been drinking heavily before he got here. I told him I had a beer in the fridge and he let me go into the kitchen."

"Was he armed?"

"I don't believe he was. I keep my cell phone on the counter. When he wasn't looking, I called the police and tried to talk to the operator. I only had a few seconds to whisper something. I just told her to listen and I kept my conversation loaded with tips on my location. The operator stayed quiet. I'd say within three minutes, the police were all over the place. Greg gave up without so much as a whimper. He just had this look on his face, like I betrayed him or something.

"When I checked the window, most of the glass was on the outside. He must have tried to remove my jalousie windows and dropped a few of them."

Anita waited patiently until I finished a sentence. I closed the notebook.

"The police want to question him in the murders of two people. Do you think Greg is capable of harming anyone?"

Anita glanced at the sea shells on the wall, then back at me. "They say stalkers rarely take their obsessions to murder. With Greg, I don't know. Just before the police arrived, he could have put his hands on my throat and that would have ended it. But he didn't. When I saw his face on the news, I kept playing that night over and over in my mind. Murder? I can't answer that."

I looked up toward Ike as a way of saying the interview was over. Ike snapped the camera from the tripod and started taking video of us sitting there. Two-shots, we called them. Ike broke down the tripod and waited for me to open the door.

"Like I said, I just hope they catch him." Anita Fulton got up to see us to the door. She pulled up the purse and eased the strap over her shoulder. "I don't go anywhere without it."

A certain air of determination settled in her face.

"I know the police are looking for him, but if he ever comes back here . . ." Anita hitched the strap up so the bag nestled into her armpit. Her hand kept patting the side of her purse.

Chapter Thirty-five

On Monday morning, I got into the office late. Ike stopped by the police station and picked up a copy of Anita Fulton's police call. He had a cassette tape player ready when I arrived in the bureau. I kept a promise not to bother Frank Walker for an interview until after lunch. It would give me time to go over the audio tape. Ike slipped the tape inside a cassette player and handed me three pages stapled together.

"They had a transcript," Ike said. He hit the play button.

I spread out the pages of written conversation on my table, and listened. The whole thing lasted only a few minutes. In some places, I couldn't understand any of the words spoken. A few seconds passed and we heard the fridge door opening and the clinking of what sounded like beer bottles. Anita could be heard whispering to the operator. In a low voice, Anita said she was being held hostage, pleading with the operator to listen and not talk. Anita gave her address. Soon, the voice in the background increased in volume. I guessed Anita carried the cell phone somewhere hidden on her body, moving closer to Wilding.

I heard what sounded like Greg thanking her for the beer, explaining why he was there, outlining a reason why he smashed the window to get inside her house. After Greg demanded for them to be together, Anita told him to get away. A scuffle was heard on the tape. Muffled voices. A plea was made by Anita for Greg to stop. There was the soft crunching of steps on broken glass. The operator yelled into the phone. Silence.

"That's the end?" I asked.

Ike nodded and hit the rewind button. "I think Greg found the phone and hung up. You want to hear it again?"

"Yes."

While Ike reset the audio tape, I called Frank Walker.

"Hello."

"Frank, first let me say thanks for the tape. But after their conversation and fight, it cuts off."

"Wilding heard something," Walker started. "Our patrol units think he heard the operator and panicked. The officers arrived three minutes later and Wilding was arrested."

"Do you know where Anita was hiding the phone?"

I heard Walker flipping through pages. A few seconds passed. "Can't help you there. If you want me to ask Collins, I'll put it on my list."

"Thanks. And Wilding's car?"

"No luck there. We haven't found it yet."

I ended the conversation. We played the audio tape four more times. During each play, I imagined the fear and desperation of Anita Fulton, confronted in her own home. Mike Brendon reached for another donut but stopped before his hand reached the box.

"I can't stop myself." He left his hand trembling above the box, in a mock showing of the donut's dominance over him. He eased his hand back to his side. "So, you've got a new angle for tonight?" His gaze drifted from the box to me.

"The tape is a good start."

Anita Fulton's home looked more appealing in the daylight. A low hedge of fine-cut ficus lined the far side of the house. The ocean was flat and the water looked perfect for boating. I knocked a few times but there was no answer, so I left my business card. I wanted to interview her about the audio tape.

* * *

When I got back to the station, a pink message slip was on my desk. William Jackels wanted me to call him. I reached his office in two rings.

"Is Mr. Jackels there? It's Matt Bowens. Channel Fourteen."

"He stepped out for a meeting. I just know he wanted to speak to you."

"When will he be back?"

"Sometime later this afternoon, possibly by three."

"Fine. Will you leave a message that I tried to call him."

"No problem." I gave her my cell phone number. After lunch I got a short interview with Frank Walker about the Fulton audio tape.

It was 3:20 P.M. when I decided to call Jackels instead of waiting for his call. The secretary said he wasn't back from his meeting and she didn't know when he would return. I gave her my cell number again and put down the phone.

Ike had my script taped to the metal rack which contained a stack of equipment to edit digital video. He reached down to adjust his chair higher, and eased his legs under the edit tray of buttons and audio controls. Two monitors rested next to each other. One monitor showed the final version, and the second displayed Ike's raw video.

"Is this where you want to start?" Ike played with the audio from Fulton's call. It was cued up to the first words from the operator.

"That's it."

The audio followed the recorded comments of Frank Walker. I tied in the current part of the investigation with a short clip from Fulton's interview along with the police call. Lankin was in another booth putting together the angle of flyers being passed out to get someone to call regarding Lane's murder. Both stories were slated for the 5 P.M. newscast.

"Play that again." My question made Ike stop and look over his shoulder.

"Here?"

"Yes. Replay that."

We sat listening as Greg argued and fought with Anita Fulton. Again, in the midst of his attack, there was the distinct sound of glass being stepped on.

"We heard that before," Ike said. "They were struggling. There was probably glass all over the place."

I thought about what Ike said. "How long is the story?"

He checked the counter. "Two minutes, twenty seconds."

Long for a television story, but the producers usually won't argue length if the story is strong. We drove back to the police station. I did a live report with my elements, and Lankin reported from the neighborhood where the flyers were passed out. I kept thinking about why Jackels tried to contact me.

Chapter Thirty-six

When I stepped into the kitchen, and put down the bag of deli sandwiches, I found the paperwork on the table. Cat didn't notice until I picked up the two pages sticking out of a folder. The list included half a dozen Mercedes Benz dealerships in the county.

"And you were going to do what?"

"At least three of them stay open late. I wanted to talk to the service department and see if Wilding had his car worked on recently. Maybe there's a receipt for another home."

"They may not talk to you. Besides I'm sure the police are looking into this. You don't have to check—"

"Yes, I do have to check. I can't just sit around and hope the police find this guy."

"They are working—"

"Why haven't we heard anything?" Cat cut me off. "I can't do anything from the office."

"When was the last time you picked up a book for your class?"

"How can I think of classes when someone murdered Stacy? I don't have the money to put up thousands of dollars on the reward, but I just—"

Tears collected in each corner of her eyes until she blinked them downward against her cheek, stopping at her lip. She wiped the streaks from her face.

"I'm done crying about this. I want to get up and get involved to find Wilding."

"Let the police—"

"Are you going to stop me?" She stood up and came at me until she looked directly into my gaze.

"No, Cat. I'm just trying to talk to you."

"Talk. That's all I hear from you. Talk."

"Mommy, can I come out now?" Jason's question was muffled by the closed door.

"No." Her eyes were different. The gleam was replaced by a controlled burn. It seemed she was no longer listening to me, but operating on another plane. My pager thumped and I checked the number.

"I've got to make a call."

Cat's expression never changed. I dialed the number.

"Hello, is this Mr. Bowens?"

"This is Pam over in Mr. Jackels' office at the summit conference. I'm so sorry to bother you, but you gave me your pager number and your cell."

"Yes, is Jackels near the phone?"

"That's just it." There was a sense of pain in her voice. "Mr. Jackels never returned from his meeting. And now the police are here, going through his office. I was told to check with you to see if you've heard from him."

"I'm sorry. I haven't," I told her. "He was due back at three?"

"Yes. When he didn't return by five, I called his cell several times."

"Anything?"

"No. So I immediately called the police. Detective Collins is here."

"I'll be right there."

Chapter Thirty-seven

In my mind, I ran through the last few conversations with Jackels, trying to come up with an idea on where to find him. I clicked on the radio and switched the dial to the all-news station. An easy-toned voice brought me up to date on the wild fires in the Everglades, and the latest on the search for Wilding.

The message from Jackels said he wanted to speak with me. About what? If there was a compelling reason to reach me, he would have called my cell. He must have felt it wasn't worth contacting the police. Or perhaps, for Jackels, this was his way of stepping away from the investigation. Just disappear. I weighed his possible involvement in the deaths of Lane and Stacy. He had control over their lives. Maybe Jackels used the connection between Priscomb and a counterfeiter to scare Lane. If Colon cost Priscomb a direct line to the oval office, maybe Jackels used the information to stalk and blackmail Lane Redmond.

The voice on the radio kicked up in volume. "We have this just in. It seems people have discovered a stash of money in the streets of south Florida. We are told Grazie Park just outside Fort Lauderdale is in bedlam right now. People are finding wads of money in the street! Don't get any ideas about going there right now, the area is blocked off and police have sectioned off the road."

The radio voice laughed hard and made a few jokes about

155

it raining money. I slowed the Beemer and stopped. I angled my cell phone into the street light to see the numbers before I dialed.

"Channel Fourteen . . ."

"It's Bowens. Tracy?"

"What's up Matt?"

Tracy's voice wobbled with the strength of someone just out of college. This was his first job in television and at times, he wasn't quite sure of himself.

"Do you have a crew at the free money grab?"

"Yes. We're going live with a special report as soon as the truck gets there."

"The reporter?"

"My night reporters are tied up on other stories. I managed to reach Lankin."

"Tell him I'm headed that way."

"It's okay Matt. Enjoy your evening—"

"Tell him!"

"No problem. Is there something else to this?"

"I don't know yet. It's just a feeling. If it's nothing, I'll back off. But let him know."

"Sure."

I made a second call before turning back into traffic. Two rings.

"Summit conference committee. Pam speaking."

"Pam, it's Matt Bowens. Any word on Jackels?"

"No. Not yet. Detective Collins was here, but he left."

"Did he say where he was going?"

"No, just that he left. If you check back tonight, I'll be gone. The answer machine will catch your call. I have to be back here early and ready in case Mr. Jackels comes in."

"I understand. Thanks."

I arrived as a man in handcuffs was led away by a uniform. Off to my right, several people were looking down at the ground. Their pace and direction were erratic.

I looked up ahead at the mosh pit of bodies pushed together. This was a free-for-all. I bumped into one man. His hand was raised into the air. A stack of one hundred dollars bills were jammed tightly between his fingers. He was screaming something I couldn't understand. Uniforms pushed into the crowd, fighting with people for the money. It was hard to hear over the din. I saw a television light and followed the beam to the camera of Kyra Gibson. She was jostled but kept her camera rock solid straight. Lankin was on top of the live truck, describing the action below. I couldn't hear or understand his words, but he kept pointing to the pandemonium.

"Welcome to the party." A face in the crowd tried to stand without getting pushed down.

"What?"

"I said . . . welcome to the party!" He shouted then stepped back into the pack. I saw Detective Collins near the Police Special Response Unit truck. The RV was only brought out for certain emergency occasions. Eighty people pushing and shoving each other over stacks of free money must have been a reason to haul it out. I worked my way to Collins, but it was like going upstream amid waves of bodies. Each time someone found a bill, it encouraged others to search the same spot. I was a few yards away from Collins when a sergeant raised a bullhorn to his mouth.

"This is the police. Please leave the area immediately. If you do not heed this warning in the next two minutes, you will be arrested. Repeat, you will be arrested."

The announcement did nothing to stop the avid search. Collins had his back to me when I finally reached him. Two perfect stacks of bills rested on the hood of his unmarked car.

"Where did it come from?" I shouted at first, but realized it was quiet enough and lowered by voice. "Was there an armored car drop or what?"

Detective Collins turned around. I could see the days of going without sleep leaving its mark on his eyes.

"Take a look at it."

I hesitated.

"Go ahead," Collins began. "Take a good look."

I peeled off the top two bills from the stack and held them

up to the light. No watermark. Still, the paper felt almost perfect.

"Check out the serial numbers." Collins watched my face for a reaction.

I checked one bill, then another. The serial numbers matched. Each bill had the same series of numbers and letters.

"They're fake," I said.

"You got it." Collins straightened a stack of bills and smacked them down on the hood of his car.

"Where did they come from?"

"The quality is the best I've ever seen. We've got our own Economic Crimes Unit down here, and the Secret Service is on the way."

"That still doesn't answer the question—"

"We don't know where they came from. At least not yet. I'm hoping the experts will tell me."

Collins turned his glance toward the crowd.

"The sergeant is about to announce this stuff is phony. The question is .'. . do you think that will stop these folks from picking up these bogus bills?"

"No."

"The stores and banks around here are going to be busy for the next year sorting this all out." Collins then angled his head toward the sky. He lifted an arm until it was pointed straight up.

"I called Fort Lauderdale tower, and so far, I've managed to keep your news helicopters away from here. If I see one helicopter blowing this stuff all over the place, I'm going to have someone's head. Is that clear?"

I felt a tap on my shoulder. Michael Ivory stepped into my stare. The spokesman for the The US Attorney's office glanced at the street then back at me.

"Getting into trouble, Bowens?" He studied the display of bills and picked up a stack. Ivory glided his ebony fingers down the paper. "Not bad. Not bad at all. This has the look and feel of Hector Colon."

Ivory put the bills on top of the stack and cocked his head at Detective Collins. "You'll have to excuse us."

They both moved behind the RV and away from my view. I looked back for Lankin. A lone tripod stood on top of the live truck. I pulled out my cell phone. Five rings.

"Channel Fourteen, please hold."

I waited a minute before he picked up the phone.

"Channel 14."

"Tracy, what's going on?"

"You won't believe the calls we're getting. Everyone wants to know the location of the money. I'm swamped. The phones won't stop ringing."

"Tell them it's counterfeit."

"You're kidding?"

"Tell them it's bogus. And that if they try and take it, they'll be arrested."

"That's too bad. You sure? I can't believe—"

"Believe it. Now what's the phone number to the live truck? I've got to talk to Lankin."

Tracy gave me the number and I dialed the truck.

"Lankin."

"Ron. It's me. Bowens. I'm across the street at the command post. When's your next report?"

"I've got another live hit in twenty minutes."

"Ron, the money is no good. It's a very good grade counterfeit. The feds are here along with Detective Collins. Anyone caught trying to take it will be arrested. Got it?"

"Got it. But it's still a crazy scene."

"I'll be there in a few minutes."

I pushed the phone back into my pocket as the sergeant again raised the bull horn to his lips and repeated the message. The money was not genuine. The response from the crowd was a loud boo. Two uniforms moved through the throng, directing people to put the money into a large box. Other uniforms stood by ready to enforce the rule. The talking began to subside.

That's when I noticed it. A sign at the southwest corner of the park. All of the money was found in the street just outside the front gate, which was locked. The huge billboard touted the opening of a new section of the park and the ribbon cutting was a day away.

I recognized the detectives. Two men and a woman dipped their heads under the sign and kept going. Detective Collins led the trio. They walked slow, looking down at the ground. Clearly, they were not looking for money. Collins stopped. I made my way to where they were standing. It didn't take them long to find something. All three aimed their flashlights at an object on the ground. My vantage point was just yards from their search, close enough to see their badges flash a gold glow every few seconds in the street light. All three shined their beams down at the face of William Jackels. His arms were down at his side and one leg was crossed over the other like the limbs of a crumpled doll. He was wearing a jogging suit. I didn't see any blood, but his eyes were locked open in a death gaze.

Collins dropped down and checked the pulse of Jackels. He stood up and took a few steps back. Now he would have to wait until the crime techs and the medical examiner finished their work. He said a few words to the investigator next to him and the detective approached me.

"Sorry to do this to you, but you're going to have to move back."

"Tell Collins to page Frank Walker and get him out here."

"Fine, fine." His words were hurried. "We've got a zillion people stomping all over a crime scene. Everyone has to get back."

"Can you confirm that's William Jackels?"

"We haven't contacted the next of kin yet. We can't confirm anything."

"Ask Collins if we can say this is tied to the investigation into the deaths of Lane Redmond and Stacy Gaines? And the work of the summit committee?"

The detective walked a slow walk away from me, but he passed on my request. Collins himself came to answer my question.

"Sorry Matt. We can't confirm much. If you want to say this might be connected, I have no problem with that. It's obviously Jackels, but we can't say that yet. Okay?"

I nodded.

"We've got a long night ahead of us. I can page Walker but he won't be here for a while."

"We'll be here." I pointed to the live truck.

"I'll send him there," he said.

Collins stood still, watching me until he saw I was stepping backward and away from the body. He raised his radio to his face. A few seconds later, I watched a uniform walk to the trunk of his car and pull out a large roll of yellow crime tape.

The counterfeit money was a cover for the murder. I ran through the gamut of facts. Three members of the summit committee were now dead. All of them killed in a public location. I watched two uniforms stuff a bucket full of fake bills. The very thing Lane, Stacy and Jackels worked against was being thrust out in the open, a deadly final slap at their effort to stop counterfeiting. Could Hector Colon be responsible for all three deaths and not Greg Wilding?

A sergeant directed stragglers to get to their cars and leave the area. By the time I reached the live truck, only a few people remained on the street. The crime scene tape stretched from several trees blocking off a wide section. Crime scene techs arrived and after taking some pictures, they covered Jackels with a tarp. A bank of high intensity lights came on.

"Okay, Ron. Everything just changed. I don't want to move in on your story, so I'll just give you the information. They just found a body in the park."

"No way?"

Lankin's eyes widened. Gibson stopped editing the latest story about the found money.

"A body? Where?"

I pointed to the county information board just to the entrance to the park.

"It's under there. We can't report it yet, but it's Jackels, the head of the summit conference."

Lankin leaned back into his seat, stunned. "What do you want me to do? I don't mind giving up the story."

"You sure?"

"You've got the edge on this. Call Miami and let them know, and I'll hit the street for any updates."

I picked up the telephone in the live truck and told producers in Miami I would do the live shot. I placed the phone back into the holder and spoke to Kyra Gibson.

"Miami says we're up and live as soon as I can get in front of the camera."

A vision of a chalk-faced Jackels, his body slipping quickly into full rigor, twisted my stomach into a slow churn. Minutes later, I looked into the camera and gave south Florida the few details I could provide. A victim with no name for now, and the link to the death of two summit staffers.

Quick flashes of Lane, Stacy and Jackels peppered my inner thoughts. I finished the live report.

"You're working some long hours." Gibson's jaw pulled downward in a look of concern. She cocked her head to the side in an attempt to move the dark locks away from her eyes.

"I'm fine."

"You getting any sleep?" Her eyes studied my face.

"Not much."

The crowd was now a trickle. A few stayed behind the crime tape, looking for a view of the body. Frank Walker arrived without a tie. The detectives were his first stop. I surveyed the area. Police kept looking for any money left behind.

Jackels was discovered at least twenty yards away on the grounds of the park, plenty of distance from the money grab. There were clear similarities with the murders. All three were left outdoors in a place about to become very public in the next few hours. I couldn't tell, but if Jackels suffered stab wounds, the scenario was the same in all three cases.

"I understand you were here when Jackels was found?" Frank Walker hand-combed a small tuft of hair back into place as he spoke.

"I had a gut feeling." I turned my wrist up for a time

check: 9:20 P.M. Plenty of time before the 11 P.M. newscast. "Did they recover most of the money?"

Walker's eyebrows bent inward. "Well, since we have no idea how much money we're dealing with, we don't know how much currency got released to the public."

"Can you officially ID the body?"

"Not yet. Give me an hour on that. We understand he has an ex-wife living in Tulsa."

"Jackels drove a black Lexus. Have you located his car?"

Walker shook his head. "We've got people heading to his condo. So far, we haven't heard."

"Any security cameras near here?"

"Only at the entrance gate, and it was closed. They shut the cameras down when they lock up."

"Who takes control of the money?"

Walker looked over his shoulder. A detective held up the tarp to block any view by photographers. Behind the tarp, two crime techs were gathering what evidence they could.

Walker turned back to me. "For now, we have the money. They might check some of it for prints, but so many people have handled it." Walker paused. "I know your next question. Was Jackels stabbed? On that, we'll have to wait for the autopsy. I'm told there were signs of trauma but I can't say what that means. I've got to get with the other reporters. I'll check back with you later."

Walker would make stops at each live truck, updating each reporter at the scene. By 11 P.M. we had most of what we would get for the night. Police officially released the name of Jackels as the victim. We would have to wait on the autopsy. The search continued for his car. A plea was made to bring in the counterfeit money. No questions asked. Lankin urged me to go home after the live report. When I left, the crime techs were still checking the ground, working and taking photographs, looking for a case breaker.

Chapter Thirty-eight

My drive to the station seemed like I was on autopilot. I found Ike sitting in his van. I waved but he didn't respond. He lowered the window as I approached. He sat there, eyes forward, flicking his car keys with his fingers, a look of dejection on his face.

"Something's been bothering you all week." I waited for a response.

Ike kept his eyes positioned on the dashboard for several seconds before he looked up. "My daughter is in college now, I've been in this business for a long time, and I talked it over with my wife." Ike kept flicking at the keys. "How do you know when it's time to quit?"

He hit the keys harder than before, then stopped.

"When you've seen enough," I told him.

"Maybe that's me." Ike pulled his hands back and stacked his arms against his chest.

"You want to talk to Brendon about it?"

"No, I'll wait. Knowing me, sometime tomorrow I'll be fired up to working the next twenty years in news." Ike squinted at me.

"You sure? We can go catch some breakfast."

"I'm fine."

I left him in the parking lot and headed for the front door. Mike Brendon gave me a second look as I eased my briefcase on the desk.

"I thought about calling you," Brendon started, "to tell you to come in a bit later. Let you get some more sleep."

"I'll be ready. Anything else happen overnight?"

"No." Brendon paused and took a sip of his coffee. "I've got Lankin back at the park. He didn't get any sleep either. The county is still supposed to cut the ribbon on the new section of the park. Right in the middle of a crime scene." Brendon raised the cup for another draw of coffee. "The scene has pretty much cleared. The body was removed and the tape is down."

Brendon rested his cup and started to laugh. "Do you believe it? There's people back out there this morning looking for money." He shook his head. "I figured I'd wait and talk to you and get some idea on how you want to proceed. I mean what do you want to do?"

I rolled my shoulders a few times to loosen the muscles in my neck. "Let me think about it. Ike's sitting in the van. Is he headed somewhere?"

"I'm going to have him stop over at the summit office to see if anyone wants to talk."

I ripped the top off two packs of sugar and poured the granules into my coffee. The phone rang and Brendon answered. After a few seconds he turned his glance toward me.

"Here. It's for you. Some guy says he has to talk to you."

"What guy?"

"Here . . . you talk to him."

I pushed a stir stick into the dark liquid and rested the mug on my calendar.

"Hello. Matt Bowens, can I help you?"

"Yes . . . I don't know where to start."

I could hear a mixture of street noise in the background. A blend of cars and voices.

"Are you talking from a pay phone? Speak up a bit."

"This is hard."

"Just tell me what you want to say." I took a sip from the cup.

"It's just that . . ." The voice paused. "I'm sorry. Let me start over. My name is Greg Wilding. And I want to turn myself in."

Chapter Thirty-nine

I snapped my finger to get Brendon's attention.

"Say that again? You say your name is Greg Wilding?"

I spoke loud enough for Brendon to hear every word. Brendon pushed back from his chair, getting to my desk in three steps. I pressed the phone hard against my ear.

"Yes." The voice on the phone was low.

"Keep your voice up if you can. The connection is pretty bad."

"I know the police are looking for me. I will only stay on the line a few seconds."

"Don't hang up! Don't hang up! Where are you?"

"First, I want some assurances."

"I can't promise anything until I hear it."

"I want a reporter there. I've watched you do the stories about this and I want to make a statement. To you, on camera."

"We can do that." I wrote the words WANTS AN ON-CAMERA INTERVIEW in large letters on my calendar. Brendon stepped back to his desk and reached for a legal pad.

"Where can we meet you?"

"Not so quick. One other thing." The voice was clear and full volume.

"I'm listening."

"I want you to go with me to the police station. Every step of the way."

"We can work that out. Where are you?"

"I'm going to get off the phone. Meet me at the Riverwalk path, just under the Third Avenue bridge, in ten minutes. If you need the exact spot, the police will tell you—"

"Where are you?"

Dial tone ended the conversation.

"He says the police knows where he is?"

"So . . . is this some kind of a hoax?" Brendon yelled.

"I don't think so."

"How did he sound?"

"Just like the voice on the nine-one-one tape."

The phone rang again. I snapped up the receiver.

"Hello?"

"Matt Bowens?" I recognized the voice of Detective Collins. "Did you just get a phone call from Gregory Wilding?"

"Yes."

"This is the way we'll play it." His voice was spiked with urgency then eased into a calculating rhythm. "Here's the situation. He claims he has someone tied up. We have several units outside the location, but we have not been inside. We were able to make contact by phone, but he insists on talking to you. Our negotiator moved our people back just a bit. Once he does the interview, he says he will free the hostage and give himself up. You can let him talk but we will be everywhere and we might move in at any time."

"How long has this been going down?"

"About fifteen minutes."

"I didn't hear anything on the scanner."

"We're on a secure channel. We could bust in there, but if we can get this done without anyone getting hurt, I'll take it. You don't have to do this."

"It's fine. I just need to get our gear set up. It will be Ike, myself and a live truck operator."

"Wilding sounds like he wants to cooperate, so we'll string this out. But if we get any notion that something's not right . . ."

"I understand."

"Go on and meet him. He's on a party boat docked under the bridge." Collins was gone.

I eased the phone down.

Details, questions and logistics tumbled through my mind like falling dominoes. "Mike, get in touch with Ike. Head him toward Riverwalk. I'll go in my own car."

I wanted to check in with Cat. The talk of a hostage bothered me. Brendon paged Ike, then started dialing again.

"I'm getting in touch with Ramirez," he said.

Before Ramirez was news director, he was a reporter for twelve years. Any final decisions on what we did rested with him and the general manager of Channel 14.

"Go!" Brendon urged. "Head there, and I'll conference the three of us on your cell phone."

The drive to the Riverwalk was five minutes away. I turned down Third Avenue and started over the bridge. My cell phone rang.

"Bowens . . ."

"It's Mike. I've got Ramirez on the line as well."

"Hello Matt." The voice of Ramirez sounded calm. "We've got a live truck rolling on this. We're going to take the whole thing live. The interview, the surrender, all of it. We'll break into programming as soon as you set up."

"You think all the activity with the truck will spook him, Matt?" Brendon's question brought up more concerns. The caller never said anything about engineers, cables, and a live audience.

"Did he say anything about the murders?" Ramirez asked.

"No. We never got that far. But I'm worried about his hostage. Do me a favor Mike. Try to reach Cat. The number is in my Rolodex."

"No problem."

The last few blocks were behind me. I guided the Beemer down Las Olas Boulevard headed west, finally reaching a spot near East Third Avenue. "I'm almost there."

There wasn't any time to look for a parking space so I jumped the curb and left the Beemer on the grass. I checked for undercover officers, but I couldn't spot anyone. I kept the phone stuck to my ear, talking as I ran from the car.

"Mike?"

"Yeah, Matt . . ."

"Any word on Cat?"

"No answer at the house. And her work line is busy."

I tried to focus on Wilding. "I know the police are going to be around, but I'm going to take a cue from Anita Fulton and leave my cell phone on until Ike arrives. You'll be able to hear just in case things get shaky."

"Sure, Matt."

A uniform stood outside his car. His hand was on his weapon and he held a radio close to his ear. As soon as he saw me, he waved me past him. I never spoke to him and kept walking away from the police car, toward the shade under the Third Avenue bridge. And the boat.

I considered more questions. What if Wilding changed his MO to a gun? Walker said the killer used a knife. I walked, mentally marking how far I'd have to go to be within shooting range. My view of the water line was blocked by a curving row of Crepe Myrtle trees at the edge of Riverwalk. Each step was gauged. The sound of car tires on the metal grid of the bridge grew louder as I reached the water. I counted at least four more police units on the other side of the river.

I clipped the phone on my belt. From left to right, Riverwalk was quiet. A man with a rolled up newspaper stepped past me. He was too old to fit the mold of a detective. The uniform waved for the man to come out of the area. Riverwalk was a linear park, made up of a paved brick pathway overlooking the waterfront, shady rest spots, and trees. I searched the walkway in both directions.

Nothing.

The water moved so slow, you couldn't get a read on which way the current was going. I stopped and stood a few yards from the pathway which hugged the water. I wanted to make myself as visible as possible. But in the midst of nearby office buildings I felt vulnerable. Wilding still had the advantage. He could be just out of reach, *stalking me*.

The cell phone gave me communication, and the police were nearby, but they yielded no protection from a quick strike. Lane Redmond must have thought she had little to guard against an attacker.

A jogger zigzagged around me. An officer? Possibly. His eyes never wandered toward me, only the path ahead. The warning ring from the bridge echoed across the top of the water. A red light flashed from below the bridge, and the long span yawned open and kept moving upward. Cars stopped. I expected to see a huge yacht ease past the bridge opening, separating the water in a crawl toward an inland marina. There was nothing. Just the bridge moving to the up position.

As the bridge stretched upward, the shadow of the span grew smaller in shape until the sun exposed the party boat to the full bore of the light. The boat was tied up and docked next to the walkway under the bridge. People would rent time and the craft drifted down the river, serving food and drinks.

The boat was in front of me. The vessel was square-sided with two levels. The second floor was probably used for dancing and live music. There were large windows. A door was closed. I walked onto the gantry but stopped midway to look back. Six or seven SWAT members took up spots along the Riverwalk. One adjusted a helmet after running into place.

"Mr. Bowens. Is that you?"

I turned around. The door was now open and the voice came from inside the boat.

"Come on in," the voice said. The deck was firm so it didn't rock when I took my first steps.

I could feel everyone watching me: The police, and man on the boat. I stepped inside. He was leaning against a wall, away from the windows and close to a door, which was in the full shadow. He was shorter than I thought. My eyes were immediately drawn to his hands. No visible weapons.

But a knife or shank could easily be hidden on the body. His jeans had small holes near the bottom of the pants. The shoes were road worn and scuffed. A strap across his chest was connected to a carry bag. He wore a faded green tropical shirt covered with tiny palm trees. And his hair was mid length. It was Greg Wilding.

"Can we sit out there?" He pointed to a bench which was off the boat.

"Out there? Are you sure?"

"I want to talk out in the open. If they're going to shoot me, they'll have to do it in front of your camera."

"Where's the hostage?"

"In time. In time. Where's your crew?"

"Coming. You want to wait for him? It will only be a few minutes." I didn't want to break my fix on his eyes, but I tried to search the boat.

"C'mon, Mr. Bowens. Let's take a chance and go outside."

"You sure about this?" I had visions of the back of my head in the cross hairs of a high-powered rifle.

"C'mon, live a little. You first."

I turned around. If he wanted to power a blade between my ribs, he had his chance. I stepped back across the sun-covered gantry. One step. Then a second. I didn't stop until I reached the bench. His eyes surveyed the office buildings nearby before centering again on me. His expression was almost one of being impatient, as if he enjoyed the spotlight. He motioned for me to sit down. I felt eyes on my back. Why didn't Cat answer the phone?

"Is the hostage on the boat?" I asked.

Wilding glanced over to the water then back.

"I told the police I have someone stashed away somewhere, and that if I don't get to talk to you, they'll never find out where that person is located."

I weighed his words and mannerisms for any sign of deception.

"I just wanted to let you know, I have some people coming," I told him. "A photographer to record this . . . a Channel Fourteen truck to put it on the air—"

"You think I'm evil. Don'tcha, Mr. Bowens?"

"That isn't for me to decide. I just want to give you what you asked for. A chance to get your side out, and to surrender."

"Have you ever killed anyone, Mr. Bowens?"

"No. I've never been put in that situation."

He examined my face, probably comparing my on-air appearance with the person sitting next to him. I looked for any sign of Ike, or the live truck.

"Would you believe me, Mr. Bowens, if I told you I wasn't that evil?" His words were measured and level, never too much of a lilt. He took his time to release each word.

"How do you define evil?" I asked.

"Oh, I think you know what I mean. You're afraid I'll strike at you right now. Don'tcha Mr. Bowens?"

Before I could answer, he posed another question.

"You have faced danger before, haven't you? I can sense it." He closed his eyes for a few seconds the way someone seeps deep into meditation. The prickly stubble of an unshaved chin turned upward to form the bottom portion of a half-smile.

"You almost died once. Am I right?"

I didn't know how to answer him. A blink in measured time and I was no longer before Wilding. I was back in Chicago preparing to cross the street into the housing project. The .45 came up and out of the rear car window. The blast threw me back against a pole and to the ground, a victim of a drive-by shooting on gang turf. The sky turned from cream to darkness. I could form a few words, but I couldn't move.

"Reminiscing, eh, Mr. Bowens?"

Over my shoulder, I caught a glimpse of Ike Cashing. He was carrying a tripod, and camera.

"My photographer is here. We'll be up and doing the interview in a matter of moments."

The live truck rolled up on the grass and parked behind my Beemer. The engineer got out and flipped the switch to bring up the microwave mast.

Ike eased the camera to the ground, and pulled out a

microphone from a bag around his waist. He clipped the microphone in place. Wilding watched with a degree of fascination. I picked up the cell phone.

"Everyone still on the line?"

"We hear every word," Ramirez began. "The police called. They're all around you. They say they are set to move in. You don't have a lot of time. I'm going up to the control booth, and I'll talk to you through your earpiece."

I put the phone back at my side. I kept it on for Brendon to keep listening.

"Afraid of losing touch with your people?" Wilding adjusted the bag on his shoulder. His quick movement made me pause and my body stiffened waiting for a barrage of gunfire. The air was quiet.

"We're just getting set up," I said. "That's all."

The engineer handed a cable to Ike then ran back to the truck and never even glanced over at Wilding. Ike hooked up the final connections to his camera. I clipped on my microphone and earpiece and waited for Ramirez to give me a countdown.

"Matt. Are you there?" The voice in my earpiece was Ramirez.

"We're set." I looked over at Ike who gave me a thumbs up.

"Okay Matt, we're set to go in one minute. Just one other thing. Our network and CNN have both asked to take our feed. You now have a national audience."

My mind wasn't on numbers. I turned toward Ike's camera.

"Okay Matt, you're hot in thirty seconds," Ramirez said in my ear.

Wilding's even smile never moved.

"Matt, we're up in fifteen seconds. New York and Atlanta can hear and see you."

Ike pulled his face from the camera one last time, probably to check the angle and how far he would need to pan to include Wilding in the shot.

"Matt . . . coming at you in five seconds."

I heard the taped opening of the announcer's voice and the words ". . . Special Report . . ."

"Good morning. I'm Matt Bowens. A search has been ongoing in south Florida and the country for Greg Wilding, who is wanted for questioning in the deaths of three people. He contacted Channel Fourteen to say he is ready to surrender to police. Before he does, Wilding agreed to answer some questions." As I turned toward Wilding, Ike panned the camera left.

"Did you kill Lane Redmond, Senator Priscomb's daughter?"

"No. I don't even know . . . I should say, I *didn't* know her."

"Were you involved in her death in any way?"

"No."

"Records show that you pleaded no contest to stalking charges and you were given probation. Police believe the victim in this case, Lane Redmond, was stalked and murdered—"

"That part may be true Mr. Bowens. I did plead no contest and I admitted in court to stalking charges, but I'm not a murderer. I did not kill Lane Redmond. I was not involved in the death of Stacy Gaines and I understand there was another murder?"

"The body of William Jackels was discovered last night."

"Again, I am stating right now, that I was not involved in any of these deaths. I did not kill those people. The reason I'm even talking right now is to get my side out there before my attorney tells me to shut up. I'm through with plea deals."

"The police say they have DNA evidence linking you to two of the murders. How do you explain that, Mr. Wilding?"

Wilding's face changed, probably contemplating the question. He remained silent. No response. Dead air.

"Again, Mr. Wilding. DNA evidence is so reliable there's a one in six million chance the sample was someone other than you. Detectives say your DNA was found at two locations on the victims." I kept fighting it down but anger crept into my voice. "How could you kill Lane Redmond? How

could you kill Stacy Gaines? It's called murder Mr. Wilding.
And the DNA is the proof!"

"I know all about DNA." Wilding's voice matched my
intensity. He paused, then brought the level of his voice back
down to a calm evenness. He took in a breath, and spoke in
an easy tone. The words were slow. Deliberate.

"I am here, ready to offer myself up to police. But Mr.
Bowens, I give you this challenge. I am not guilty.
Regardless of the DNA. The challenge for you is to deter-
mine if I'm telling the truth."

Blurs and movement caught the right side of my periph-
eral vision. Three uniforms, guns drawn approached from
my right. Behind them, Detective Collins. At least another
dozen police cars blocked the roadway. Flashing blue and
red lights reflected off the alpine-white Channel 14 live
truck. The uniforms stopped their approach. Only Detective
Collins kept a steady walk toward the bench.

"Where were you when Lane Redmond was killed?" I
asked.

Wilding reached for his backpack and pushed his hand
inside. Collins and the uniforms took direct aim with their
weapons.

"Put your guns down! It's all right!" I could feel the muscles strain in my neck. When I looked down, I was standing.
My arms thrust skyward. Hands raised. Palms outward. I
yelled, "Don't shoot!"

The uniforms did not move. The guns stayed trained at
the back of Wilding's head. I sat down on the bench, and
locked on his stare.

"Please. I know you didn't contact me just to commit sui-
cide by cop. Leave the bag here for the police. I will tell
them what you want them to know. But don't . . . repeat
don't make a move like that again."

My glance went upward. The roofs were lined with sharpshooters. A few drivers were out of their cars on the bridge.
They leaned over the railing. No one came out of the office
building.

I couldn't see them but I imagined workers pointing fingers against the tinted windows. No joggers. Boat traffic was quiet. The whole area was shut down. Wilding eased off the strap until the bag sagged against his back.

"Thank you. Again, the question. Where were you?"

"I can't go into my bag to show you." He paused in frustration. "I'm an alcoholic Mr. Bowens. I drink to the point that I black out. There are periods in my life that are missing. Gone. But in the last few days, I've been getting help."

"You can prove that?"

"I found a quiet location in Palm Beach county."

"And that's where you've been?"

"You can check for yourself."

"Why are you coming forward?"

"Why run? Where am I going? When I realized I was wanted by police, I didn't exactly know what to do. I came back into the county, and I called you."

"Are you ready to surrender?"

"There's just one thing." Wilding turned from me and stared directly into the camera. "You can't save me after they execute me." There was an eerie look of pleasure in the way his smile lined his face. "And just so you know. I'm not keeping anyone hostage. This was just a way to get my interview."

Wilding stood up, and raised his hands. Detective Collins and two uniforms moved in. It was Collins who placed the cuffs on him. I stood up and moved out of the way. Ike unhooked his camera from the tripod and stepped forward, still recording just inches from Wilding.

"Police are arresting Gregory Wilding," I began. "He has been wanted by police for questioning, and right now he is being taken into custody for the deaths of two, and perhaps three people."

Collins gave a soft yank on the cuffs as if to make sure they were secure. "Mr. Wilding, I'm placing you under arrest."

Wilding straightened his spine. He had his back to me. A police car approached us.

"You have the right . . ."

Wilding angled his head toward me until I could see the full width of his smile. If he was afraid, he didn't show it. He willingly stepped to the car. Collins held a firm grip on the plastic cuffs. Wilding appeared ready for this moment.

". . . to remain . . ."

Wilding kept his eyes toward the camera.

". . . silent . . ."

He formed words, but I didn't hear him. I stepped closer and listened.

"My attorney," he shouted. Detective Collins was about to lower Wilding's head to enter the police car. "My attorney is a public defender."

The car drove off, lights flashing. A trail of units followed. I turned back to Ike and gave a four-minute recap of what happened. Every now and then I glanced at my monitor to see pictures of Lane and Stacy and I spoke briefly about each person. On my left, a car horn urged a driver to get going on the bridge. The bridge was down and traffic was moving again. People left the office building and gathered near the live truck. The roofs were clear of sharpshooters. The street was again full of nine-to-fivers.

Chapter Forty

"The network wants you for a live talkback to New York at six-oh-three." Mike Brendon held up a stack of pink telephone messages. "They're all calling. Radio shows, news magazines."

"I don't think so." I took Brendon's smile away.

During the drive back to the bureau, I sized up a list of contacts to make. The coffee was still fresh and I took the first sip, tilting the blinds in the window, bending them upward until I could see the bay.

"Mike, as soon as I finish this coffee, I've got a few people to check out. If we get it all done in time, tell them I'll do the talkback."

"Matt, this is the network."

"They have the tape, they can run it without me, and line up some criminologist. They don't need me."

I released the blinds as my telephone rang.

"I'll get it," Brendon volunteered. I listened to him, then he apologized and hung up. "Another interview request," he said.

"I don't have time for this. I know Capers isn't going to sit around."

My pager went off and the number to Frank Walker's office appeared. I reached for my cell phone.

"Matt here. What's up Frank?"

"I just want us to be clear about something. We arrested

178

Greg Wilding for violating his probation. That's it. No murder arrest."

"Is that coming soon?"

"It's up to homicide. We have not changed from our original statement, and that is Wilding was wanted for questioning."

"And he's cooperating?"

"Not really. He won't say a word. This guy hasn't checked in with the probation office for weeks. He was transported to the jail for his violation hearing and the case continues."

"Any idea when that will be?"

"Not soon enough," Walker said.

I filed a three-minute report for the noon. Ike rolled through a fast food restaurant and we headed the forty-five miles north into Palm Beach County.

"What was he talking about?" Ike jammed a chicken sandwich into his mouth and drove with one hand.

"Wilding?"

"Yeah. He sounded so sure. And all that stuff about rehab."

Less than an hour into the drive, Ike pulled off Interstate 95 and headed toward Military Trail. First Alternative Rehabilitation was three stop lights away and due south. A green Mercedes Benz was parked outside the front door. Ike parked and carried our lunch wrappers to a garbage can.

"Welcome," said a man whose white hair and beard contrasted against his black skin. I guessed he was around seventy. Possibly older.

"Gerard Dorsey." He shook my hand. A Palm Beach County patrol car pulled up next to the Mercedes.

"That's Greg's." Dorsey pointed to the car. "The police are going to impound it for evidence. The county is here to hold it for Detective . . . Detective—"

"Collins?" I said.

"Yes. A Detective Collins called me soon after your broadcast."

"How did Wilding get to Fort Lauderdale?"

"I drove him in my car. Can we go inside? The only reason I'm talking to you is because Greg instructed me to answer your questions." Ike was ready with his gear. The glass door led to an open area. Rows of tables were lined end to end across the room.

"That's our dining hall," There was a glint of pride in Gerard's voice. "Over here we have our consultation rooms, where the staff talks with our guests. We don't call them clients here." Ike set up his camera, and indicated the camera was recording. I posed the first question.

"Did Wilding give you any indication he could be capable of murder?"

"I can only tell you what I see, Mr. Bowens. Gregory Wilding was and is a person who needs special care. I can't answer that question directly."

"The police are looking into—"

"I don't care what the police are checking. I only know Gregory had a rough time with his alcohol addiction. He obsessed over a person some time ago and during that whole time until now, the bottle took over."

"Did that obsession with people occur again?"

"When Gregory came to us, he didn't use the name Wilding. He used an alias. We don't have a television in this entire building and I don't get the newspaper. We keep the communication down to one thing. Getting over the power of the bottle."

I listed the dates of the murders and waited for a change of expression on Gerard's face.

"He was here on those dates. But I have to be honest . . . the police spoke to me briefly with the same questions. They will be here to get my statement."

"The dates, Mr. Dorsey."

"Again, one reason I'm talking to you is because Gregory signed a special waiver, giving me permission to speak. In fact, he insisted on me talking to you. But I worry . . . I don't want to hurt his case."

"Was he here on those dates?"

"He was, but you have to understand, he slipped up a few times."

"Drinking?"

"Yes. A couple of times we found him slumped over in his car. The floorboard was loaded with empties. Vodka, beer."

"Did you confiscate the car keys?"

"No."

"You report him to his probation officer?"

"We're not that type of place. We don't hold anyone and we don't get people in trouble. We didn't know anything about Wilding being wanted by the police until he told me to drive him to the next county."

"So, it's possible he could have left and confronted Lane Redmond, Stacy Gaines, or William Jackels?"

"I told you. I only know what I see. What motive would he have? But I will say this. Toward the end, and in fact last night, he was sober."

"Last night?"

"I couldn't account for all of his time, but he didn't drive his car."

"You're sure?"

"As best as I can be."

Chapter Forty-one

Ike set up his camera and shot several angles of the car before a tow truck driver hooked up the Benz for the trip to the crime lab. Several photographers were there. Frank Walker would have to repeat his comments a few more times for reporters. I called Brendon.

"Anything up?"

"Anita Fulton called. Since Wilding is in jail, she's willing to talk again."

"Thanks Mike. We'll head to Fulton first."

Anita Fulton was waiting for us. Her hands rested on her purse. "I am so glad they got him. When are they going to charge him with murder?"

"I'm not sure about that."

"What are they waiting for?"

"One thing I'd like for you to do. Could you show me where you fought with Wilding?"

"Sure."

She stood under the archway between the living room and the kitchen.

"You were here and where was the cell phone?"

Ike followed our movements with the camera.

"It was next to that sea shell on the counter, near the broken window. He paid so much attention to that beer, he never saw the phone."

182

"And during the struggle, was there any broken glass over here?"

"No. All the glass was like I said . . . by the window, outside."

"No glass inside the house? You're sure about that?"

"Yes. There was a mess out there. The jalousie windows were shattered. What are you getting at?"

"Nothing yet."

Three more questions about the arrest of Wilding, and I finished the interview with Fulton. I thanked her and we left. Ike adjusted the air-conditioning to cool the van.

"Let me stop by the office for a quick second," I said.

When we reached the bureau, Brendon pointed to another stack of messages on my desk. "One message that's not in that pack is from the police department. They plan to subpoena the entire interview. Our attorney already said anything that was on the air is theirs."

Brendon's face turned serious. "There is some talk they might want to put you on the witness stand before the grand jury."

"What did our attorney say?"

"Well, she says she will argue against that in court. You didn't witness a crime and the videotape of the interview speaks for itself."

"Anything else?"

"Lankin is getting an interview with Frank Walker on the arrest."

"Anything more?"

"That's it."

Ike yelled my name from an edit booth in the back. I made my way inside the tiny room and closed the glass door.

"You got it set up?"

"Just where you told me." Ike turned up the volume. "I isolated the sound and put it on a loop. There must be six or seven of the same sound in a row."

"Play it."

Ike hit the button. He had removed the sound of the

struggle between Anita and Greg. Now we only heard the distinct sound of breaking glass.

"Okay," I said getting closer to the speaker. "Was it breaking glass or . . . play it again."

Ike recued the string of glass sounds. We heard them all one more time. "It's not breaking glass, it might be breaking glass at the beginning but later, it's more like someone stepping on glass. Hear that?"

We listened again. A loud breaking sound was followed by the voices of Greg and Anita, then a minute later there was a softer crunch. Then another. "Those are footsteps," I said.

"You saw the spot where they were fighting? There was no glass there," I said. Ike sat, ready to play the tape a third time. "Someone else was there that night. Someone who was just outside, standing on the broken window panes looking in and watching the entire thing."

"Any ideas?" Ike ejected the tape.

"Go down the list. It doesn't make sense right now for Redmond's ex Jerry to be there. Or Jackels for that matter."

"You ready to go?"

"Not yet."

"Imagine," Ike began. "A stalker being stalked."

Ike's off comment had a lot of truth to it. What if someone followed Wilding? There was plenty of time to get away before police arrived. The concrete walkway around Anita's house could easily hide the sound of footsteps. Add the sound of the sea. And during the commotion, they might not notice a face at the window watching a drunken Greg Wilding.

"Ike, I need to do one other thing." I went to my desk and pulled the interview with the fisherman who found Stacy's body. Ike moved to one side to let me work the controls. I cued up his interview and hit the button.

The fisherman said: "We didn't see anything, just truckers rolling by." Ike gave me a blank expression. The man continued. "Just the normal run of cars, a cab, and a few trucks."

I played the last part again.

"We got enough time to do all this?" Ike said.

"No problem."

I put back the videotape and approached Brendon. "I need another favor Mike. See if you can reach Pam at the summit office. Jackels was trying to get in touch with me for some reason. If the police haven't convinced her not to talk, maybe we can try to speak with her."

The afternoon was a blur. I put together three separate stories for newscasts. Channel 14 ran long clips of the interview with Wilding, then I was debriefed on my reaction. When it was over, I tapped the numbers on the phone and waited for the ring. Dinner would have to be mixed with business.

Chapter Forty-two

"What you want now?" Rollo's thick Jamaican accent took me to a place in my mind of clear blue water and white sandy beaches. "Thanks for dinner," he said. "You can buy me jerk chicken and rice any day."

I waited until we left the restaurant to go over my questions.

"I just need your help." I eased the pad from my waist.

"I thought about what you asked me." Rollo rubbed his temples. "I run more than two hundred cabs and you want me to remember where they went one particular day?"

"If you can. It's important."

"After you called, I checked the computer. As far as I can tell, we didn't have any cabs running out near the Everglades."

"No mistake?"

"Well, Matt, I can always be mistaken. But trust me on that. No cabs were out there."

"What about another company? You're not the only one in the book."

"We go out west more than any other cab company. I'm proud to say it. You can check around, but that is our territory. We *own* it."

A couple pushed open the doors of the restaurant and Rollo stopped talking until they went by. "I helped you one time with a passenger, and that turned out to be good old Mr. Redmond. Sorry, I can't do it this time. No cabs out there."

I walked him to my Beemer. The car was parked in a lot full of rental cars. "What do you do with old cabs?"

"Old cabs?" He looked confused. "Let me think."

"They've got to be somewhere?"

"If they survive the streets. If they're not totaled, or resold out of the country, then they might end up at Lennie's Auto Auction."

I wrote down the name and repeated aloud to make sure I heard it right.

"Try Lennie's. He takes in old police cars, cabs, service vehicles. Everything."

"Thanks."

No one answered the phone at Lennie's Auto Auction. I kept driving anyway. Rush hour was over and westbound interstate traffic was gone. Darkness edged the clouds in a red tinge, and the sun was a drop of spilled wine.

I reached the gate and opened the door of the Beemer to dust wisps and the rattle of chains. A man was putting on a lock.

"Are you Lennie?" I tried to catch him before he left. A truck, with its driver's side door open. The engine hummed a soft rumble.

"There is no Lennie."

"But the sign says—"

"It's Sam."

"Sam?"

"Just Sam. Lennie sold out years ago. How can I help you?" He tugged on the lock one last time and let the chains hit the metal fence. Over his shoulder, a huge sign said:

I DON'T BELIEVE IN CALLING THE POLICE.

Under the words was a picture of a snarling dog. I couldn't see them but I knew the dogs were somewhere on the lot.

"I was looking for the owner."

"That's me. The next auction is two days from now. You can look over the cars ahead of time, starting tomorrow morning at nine A.M."

"I'm looking for used cabs. You have any?"

"A few. We don't get many. For yourself or to ship out?"

"My name is Matt Bowens. I'm with Channel Fourteen. I'm interested in anyone who bought a cab recently."

"Bowens, huh? I thought you looked familiar. I sold plenty of them in the last few weeks."

As he spoke, a guard dog stepped off an easy pace around a banged up Ford, stopped and stared in my direction.

"He won't harm you." He smiled. "Unless you step on the other side of that fence."

"Don't worry. I won't. What about the cab sales? Do you have a list I can check?"

"I can help you up to a certain point. I can talk in general about what I sell on the lot, but I can't let you see my books. Sorry."

"I don't want to see them, just tell me . . . if I came back with a few pictures, could you let me know if the face resembles someone who bought a cab here recently?"

"Mister, I can't remember my shirt size without pulling it out of my pants and taking a good look. Sorry."

"Where are the cabs?"

"Don't have any right now. I call 'm knockoffs. The logo gets painted over, but you tell the company. We have people who buy them with the ads and everything."

The dog gave up on me and sauntered to a spot under a van.

"I'm sorry Matt, I can't remember faces. People here give me fake names, wrong addresses, but I don't care. I just want the cash. My wife is waiting on me."

Sam left. I examined the cars on the lot. I tried to get a mental picture of the crime scene outside Lane's home. Her car had a flat tire. Unless she called Stacy or someone at the office, where else could she get a ride that easy? A cab. And if she didn't call a cab, maybe one was waiting for her. A knockoff. A cab driven by a murderer.

Chapter Forty-three

"The bond hearing lasted three minutes." Ron Lankin walked into the office, carrying a videotape.

"How did Wilding look?" I stirred the sugar in my coffee.

"Guilty." Lankin placed the tape on Mike Brendon's desk. "That coffee fresh?"

I nodded.

"So we're about ready to move on, this one's about over." Lankin stood in the corner of the room, behind a partition. When he spoke, his words had a slight echo.

"Matt doesn't think it's over." Brendon rolled his eyes at the ceiling.

"What else is there to do? This sucker is wrapped," Lankin said. "Wilding is caught and tied up until they put the murder charge on him." Lankin emerged from the corner with his fingers interlaced around a cup as if to warm up his hands.

"Technically, he's not charged with murder yet." I directed my words to the open room. "All they have Wilding on is the probation violation. That's it. They've got DNA and so far, nothing else. Maybe the police won't talk about connections to Wilding because there aren't any."

The room went silent. Brendon glanced at the scanners then back to me.

"We're doing a follow-up," I started. "DNA, an interview or two, that's it."

"You need me?" Lankin asked.

Brendon looked at Lankin. "The noon needs a minute-thirty hit from you on the bond hearing." Brendon was hitting his computer keyboard hard enough to make Lankin's eyes blink.

I rested my coffee mug on his desk. "You find out anything?"

"So far, nothing," Brendon said.

"What are you checking?" Lankin took up a chair.

"I've got Mike going into the BodyTracer computer program. I gave him a list of names to see if it comes back with the owner of a used cab."

"Okay Matt. And the list includes?" Lankin took a long draw from his cup.

"The living and the dead. Jackels, Jerry Redmond, Senator Priscomb."

The lines in Lankin's face bunched up. "Where are you going with this?"

"It's just something I need to check out."

"And so far?" Lankin spoke, waiting for Mike to finish the sentence.

"So far, there's nothing. No matches."

"That doesn't mean anything. Why don't you expand the list. Pop in any name we interviewed since this started."

I picked up my cup and drained the rest of the coffee. "You could still buy the car under a company name, a wife's name, through a friend. It doesn't have to be a direct line."

"But even if there's a match, what does it have to do with murder?"

I let Lankin's question linger. The stillness in the room remained until Ike backed through the front door, carrying a tripod. "This dude needs some work. I put a tag on it for engineering to take a look at it. I'll work off my shoulder."

For Ike, off the shoulder meant keeping the camera steady on his shoulder while shooting video. "Are we set to go anywhere soon?"

I reached into my drawer for a fresh writing pad. "Yes. Senator Priscomb is talking."

* * *

"I have a brief statement to make, and there will be no follow-up questions. Please respect my request on that." Senator John Priscomb stepped in front of the microphones at exactly 11:31, outside the police station. The weight of Lane's death collected in his eyes. They looked heavy from a lack of sleep. Behind Priscomb, Jerry Redmond glared at the wall of cameras and reporters.

"I just wanted to thank the police for the way they have handled this case to date." Priscomb fought with the wind to keep the paper flat so he could read the words. "I know Lane would want me to keep vigilant. And keep supporting the police until they have made an arrest. I know Mr. Wilding is in jail, and while they have not charged him in my daughter's death, we know it's only a matter of time before we can get some closure in this case. Thank you."

Priscomb and Redmond turned away from the questions being shouted. The two men marched toward a waiting car and got inside. A semicircle of reporters stood silent.

My desk telephone was ringing when I placed the videotape on my desk. I placed the tape marked PRISCOMB INTERVIEW on top of the stack.

"Hello, it's Matt."

"I see you talked to my man Greg?"

"Who is this?"

"You walked all through my house once. It's O."

"I remember you."

"I know he's a bit on the strange side. I just thought you should know the police came back."

"With another warrant?"

"Yep. They went searching again. Asked me a few questions. That kind of thing."

"Like?"

"They're trying to line up the dates. You know, when did he crash here."

"What did you tell them?"

"What I told them before. The same thing I told you. He hasn't been here. Period."

"But he has been there."

"Okay. But not recently. You know what I mean."

"What about the warrant?"

"They went through my bathroom and cleaned me out."

"What did they take?"

"Well, for one thing they took my comb, although I don't have much use for a comb anymore."

I jotted down the information: dates, new search warrant.

"As far as you know, did Greg drive another car?"

"Just the Mercedes. When he wrecked one, he got another one. Why would he drive anything else?"

"Did you ever see him in a different car? Say, a car that used to be a taxicab?"

"Your questions are beginning to scare me. No. No cab."

"Are the police still there?"

"No. They left this morning. I tried to call you, but they were watching me."

"What did they take from the other room? It should have been on the search warrant."

"I really don't have a clear idea of what they were doing. But they did ask me a few times about the other bathroom and where Greg kept his personal stuff, and about the burglaries.

"What do you mean?"

"I spent so much time worrying about my television being taken, I didn't think about it at the time. I didn't think it was important. But it was odd. It was the other thing the burglar took each time. Greg kept replacing them. I think he bought two of them."

"What was that?"

"A hairbrush."

Frank Walker entered the news bureau like he was inspecting the place. He shook Mike's hand but he kept his eyes roaming, surveying the layout of the room.

"We're back here." I cocked my head toward the last edit bay. Walker followed into the tight quarters. The equipment took up half the space. I leveled a finger at Ike Cashing. "I'm sure you know Ike. He's got the tape cued up for us."

Walker's face was rigid and serious, the way a police offi-cer might look on the witness stand.

"So, what is this again Matt? You weren't real specific on the phone." Walker watched Ike work the controls of the editing tray.

"This is the nine-one-one tape you gave me. We'll play a portion of the tape, then we'll play you the isolated sound. We want you to listen and tell us what you think."

"That's fine."

Ike hit the play button and Walker heard the portion of the tape with Wilding arguing with Anita Fulton. The volume of the fight decreased just a bit as they moved away from Anita's cell phone, but the screams were still very audible. In the middle of the assault we heard something on broken glass.

"Now, this is the isolation sound," Ike said.

Walker listened to the sound of the glass breaking, the assault in the room, then the crunching noise. His expression did not change.

"That's it." Ike hit the stop button.

"Here's what you can tell Collins," I began. "Anita had her struggle yards away from the broken glass. The glass was outside the house. We listened to this several times. We believe there was another person there. Someone on the out-side, stepping all over the broken glass and getting his kicks watching this whole thing unfold."

"Let me hear it again." Walker stepped a few inches closer to the speakers. Ike played the isolation two more times. Walker's face didn't give me a hint to what he was thinking.

"Well, thanks for bringing it to my attention. It's some-thing I will pass on to Collins."

"And it's all right to talk to you about the search warrant at the home of a Mr. Banyan?"

"Sure."

Ike picked up his camera. We stepped out into the center of the room. The camera was on.

"What were you looking for at the house?"

"This is still on ongoing investigation, even though Mr.

Wilding is in custody for violating his probation. We searched the home of his friend, Mr. Olton Banyan, and we checked for certain items that may be pertaining to the case."

"What items?"

"I can't really go into that at this time, but the detectives are still building a case."

"Is Greg Wilding going to be charged with murder today or anytime soon?"

"We afforded Mr. Wilding a chance to speak with us. He declined, even though he decided to go on national television. We will continue to do our job and reach a conclusion in this case."

"Can you confirm you were looking for a hairbrush?"

"No, not at this time."

"Did you find Wilding's hair at the crime scenes? His DNA?"

"Again, I can't get into specifics."

"It seems like this case really revolves around the DNA evidence at the scene. Did you find anything to bolster your case?"

"DNA is a key component in any investigation. All you have to do is look at crimes solved by the Cold Case unit. Those are twenty-year-old cases or more. And most of them are solved with DNA mainly because of good evidence-keeping practices back then and now."

"We just played a portion of the nine-one-one tape. And the isolated sounds that could be another person at the house. Any reaction?"

Walker kept his eyes level. His voice never showed emotion. "It's something we will look into, but I can't say anything more about that right now."

Ike was just about finished with my 6 P.M. story. I bundled Senator Priscomb's statement, along with the interview of Frank Walker about the search warrant and the missing hairbrush. Another thirty seconds were added to the story to add the angle about the broken glass sound in Anita Fulton's home.

Lankin was in the rear of the newsroom interviewing someone. I stepped closer. Wayne Poplin was sitting opposite the camera, answering Lankin's questions.

"I was really hoping I could do some work for the committee," Poplin said. "I was really counting on this to get my firm off the ground and conduct all the public relations work for the conference."

"And if the conference is put off, or disbanded?"

"I think we had a good chance of landing the event in south Florida. I'm sorry for the lives lost, but I would have been honored to represent the work and goals of the group."

Interview over, Poplin edged toward me. "Any word on the investigation?"

"It's at a critical point."

"Let me know if I can help." He pulled a new stick of gum from his pocket and turned toward the door.

Lankin approached. "Matt, you've got to come see this. It's in the first edit bay." I followed him. Ike was in the next edit bay finishing the edit on my story. Mike closed the glass door behind us.

He rested his finger on the play button.

"Our guys didn't shoot it. A stringer got this video. It came down as a video feed from West Palm Beach."

Mike pressed play.

On the television monitor I saw a man slumped up against a wall. Crimson lines dripped down the wall and collected in large pools near his torso. Red irregular-shaped stains covered his shirt.

"We're not going to air this part," Mike said. "Later on, there's video of the body covered. We can use that part."

"Who is the victim?"

"This isn't related to your story but the producers want you to make a phone call and get some information. You were the one who first brought this to our attention. I mean . . . the counterfeiting indictment."

Mike stopped the tape. "The victim is Hector Colon."

Chapter Forty-four

I edged my wine glass across the table linen, closer to Cat's glass until they both clinked.

"More?" I raised the bottle of wine into the full glow of the candle light. She pinched her fingers close together.

"Just a bit."

The pour blended in with the chatter in the room. Off to my right, a piano player tapped the first few notes of "Misty." A couple shared a joke. Soft voices spoken in the shadows of the Landscape Restaurant.

"This place hasn't changed." Cat let her glance drift around the room until she caught me staring at her. "What?"

I put my hand over her wrist. "Don't worry about the time."

"It's just that the kids—"

"Forget about the time."

I slid my hand from her wrist into her palm until our fingers locked. Her legs were crossed and I could just see the tip of a shoe dangling from her toes.

"I'm just glad we could take a moment. It's been . . ."

I didn't finish the sentence. There had to be a moment to sidestep pain and the loss of Stacy Gaines. The video of Hector Colon raised questions, but it would have to wait until morning. I pointed to the bar stools near the entrance of the Landscape.

"Was it the last chair or the next-to-last?"

Cat studied the stools. Her stare lingered there.

"The last one. That's where you were sitting when I first met you."

She smiled.

Her skin blushed bronze then chestnut in the uneven light. With her free hand, Cat played with her glass, moving it in circles and sending the wine into a rolling swirl.

"I just keep thinking," she whispered. "I want this thing to be over. Charge Wilding with murder, and get him to trial."

I let the words drift over me without a response. Wilding was a subject I was trying to avoid. Cat stopped the movement of her glass. "And your story today. Are you trying to convince people Wilding is not responsible?"

"I'm just trying to air all angles. I have to do that. If there's some doubt, we should explore it."

"Doubt? There's no question he killed Stacy and Lane. Why can't you see that? You sound more like his lawyer."

"Then why haven't the police charged him? There's got to be a reason. I didn't get the impression Wilding ever came close to Stacy. And he was in rehab."

"Matt, he could have left the compound anytime he wanted to go. You know that. He had access to a car, and probably a way to get money."

"Not much. Wilding was out of work."

"He's a stalker!" Cat's voice was almost a yell. She jerked her hand from mine. The man sitting at the next table rolled his eyes in our direction. Cat dropped her hands under the table as if to put on her shoe, then eased back into the chair until her shoulders were rigid. She placed her empty glass on top of the menu.

"Cat, I was just sizing up everything—"

"You're going to let Wilding walk away from this. He practiced on Anita Fulton and hunted down Stacy and Lane. And then he killed Jackels. Someone has to stop him." Her eyes chilled with anger. I glanced back at a room of turned heads. A waiter started to approach. Cat burned a look in his direction and he backed up.

"I'm doing my best to get at the truth," I said.

"The baby-sitter was kind enough to stay late, but I want to leave. Right now. If you won't stand up for Stacy, I will."

Chapter Forty-five

Mike Brendon positioned himself in front of four televisions. "Look at that. Every station broke into programming with the same story."

On each newscast, helicopters with mounted cameras, showed brush fires rising from the floor of the Everglades. A Channel 14 helicopter beamed back pictures of the flames moving closer to US 27, and a western unpopulated section of the county. Fire crews remained on the highway.

I picked up the phone to call Cat at work, then decided against it. Ike and Lankin were sent to the fire to check out a report cows had broken through a fence and were wandering across the highway.

"They're going to make a decision at noon," Mike said. "If the fire continues to get too close, then they'll close down the road. People driving on US 27 can't see through all that smoke." Brendon took up a seat in front of his computer and bit into a donut. "I'm going to enter these last few names into BodyTracer."

I raised a coffee mug. The coffee was cold and I went for a fresh cup. The phone call stopped me.

"Hello?"

"I'm sure you saw what happened to my counterfeiting target?"

"Ivory?"

"Yeah, it's me. If I sound depressed it's because we were

199

so close to bringing in Hector Colon on our own but someone got to him first. I was just calling to say thanks for getting his picture out there."

"No problem. So, for you it's over?"

"Not quite. We're still working through some loose ends,
and we have a good direction on who killed Colon."

"Anything I can air soon?"

"Not yet. But our agency is working with the local police.
When we have something, we'll make a joint statement."

Conversation over, I again tried for the coffee. I checked
the time: 10:17 A.M. Cat's words at dinner wore on me. It
would have been easy for Wilding to get away but I guessed
there would have to be a bed check at night. But if Wilding
knew the routine of the staff, he could easily work within the
times. The quiet-running Benz might not be heard. He could
drive one county to the south and hunt down Lane Redmond.

"Matt!" Mike shouted. "Don't you hear your phone?"

I picked up the line.

"Hello Matt, it's GG. I'm worried about Cat." I recognized the hearty voice of Cat's friend from childhood.

"What's going on?"

"The school called me. Shauna is not feeling well. They
said they called Cat and couldn't reach her. I'm the second
person on their contact call-list so they phoned me."

"Maybe Cat was away from her desk?"

"No. I called the bank. They said she never came into
work today."

"Did you try her at home?"

"No answer." She paused. "I think that's the school calling me on the other line. I've got to go pick up Shauna. I
hate to bother you at work—"

"No, that's okay."

"It's just that I'm kind of worried. Can you check on Cat
while I get Shauna?"

"No problem." There was a slight tremble in my hand setting the cup down. I made the routine phone calls to retrace
GG's efforts. No answer at home and a man at Cat's job said
she didn't call in sick. I had to find her.

"Mike, they're having a problem locating Cat. I've got to run out for a few minutes. That okay?"

"Sure, go." He continued to type away at the computer.

I moved behind the wheel of the Beemer. I-95 traffic was easy at this time of the morning. If Cat wasn't at home or work, I tried to think of where she might be. I reached her driveway in fifteen minutes. Her car was parked in its normal spot. I got out of my car. I was used to hearing music filtering from the open windows. The hood of her car was propped up, a signal something was wrong mechanically. I knocked on the door.

Nothing.

I walked around the house. Each open window I passed gave me another cringe. She always kept the place too accessible for an intruder.

The backyard was quiet. I peeked through the sliding glass doors. The remnants of breakfast were on the kitchen table. I saw spilled breakfast cereal, white dots of milk on the floor, and Jason's squirt gun rested against a chair. My thoughts kicked back to the argument with Cat. We had arrived back at her house in silence. I went back to the front door.

That's when I saw it.

The car was faded gray, the shade of primer, and parked on the swale. It wasn't there when I arrived. I stepped along the side of the house taking in more of the car. An unmarked cab. I couldn't see the driver's side but something was on the roof. My pager went off. It was Mike Brendon. The number had 911 next to it. I reached for my cell phone.

The neighborhood looked deserted. No cars. People at work. The car was blocked by my Beemer. Each step revealed more. There was a soot-gray tint covering each window to match the gray primer. The logo of the company was painted over. I punched in the numbers to reach Mike.

He picked up on the first dial.

"Matt, I finished the list with BodyTracer. You won't believe whose name showed up. The car was purchased last summer from the cab company and auctioned off—"

"What name? The car is right in front of me!" I yelled into the cell phone. The driver's side of the car was within reach. The window was down and I peeked inside the car.

"Mike. Get this! The car belongs to—"

A hand knocked my cell phone out of my grasp. It hit the driveway and rolled somewhere under the cab.

"Mr. Bowens!"

My head snapped in the direction of the two figures in the back seat. One person had his face covered with something. On his right was Cat.

"Get in, Mr. Bowens, and drive," the voice said.

I hesitated.

"Get in!"

The outline of a knife gave little reflection in the darkened light of the makeshift cab. The knife handle rested firmly in a black gloved hand. The blade tip was angled just under Cat's chin.

"You ever see the damage after a knife is thrust up and into the jaw cavity?" The voice sounded familiar but there was a strange twist in the delivery of each word. The figure laughed. A dark material covered his face. Cat squirmed in the seat. Her eyes were gripped with fear. He wore a sweat-pocked baseball cap, and blue jean jacket.

"Get in, Mr. Bowens, and drive like you own this car."

I settled behind the wheel and tried to get a fix on the person in the back seat.

"Eyes ahead please. No looking back here. That's not fair."

"Where are we going?"

"Just drive west, toward the fires."

I put the car in drive and eased down the street. I was hoping a neighbor would walk out, or see the strange car from a window. No curtains moved. The front doors remained shut. The figure put something up and under the face cover. He leaned over to me, close, like an executioner before the taking.

"She's been told if she talks, she dies. So don't try to communicate with her." He eased back into the seat.

I couldn't see a killer, but I recognized the smell.

The scent was there until it mixed with the dry winter air gusting through the window. The sweet drift of chewing gum flashed a name in my mind.

"Wayne Poplin. You don't have to do this. We can stop right now and you can let us out." My eyes flicked to the back seat then back to the road. A smile formed beneath the mesh cover.

"Very good Matt. I'm so used to wearing this when I . . . work. I think we'll keep driving."

The blade was so close to her skin. I drove around bumps, desperate to keep the ride smooth. Pretending to check the rearview mirror, I looked for something to use as a weapon.

The glove box.

Maybe there was a screwdriver, or an air pressure gauge inside the compartment. I could use it if I got close to him. I thought about the sharp pointed keys in the ignition and the pen in my pocket. But Cat could be in jeopardy before I reached Poplin and the knife.

The cigarette lighter was missing. Another glance at the back seat. The door lock on Cat's side looked altered.

"Eyes ahead. Don't make me tell you again!"

He was still talking through the thin netting covering his face.

"Why are you doing this?"

Silence.

We entered State Road 595 and joined westbound traffic. Tall columns of black smoke clogged half the sky. Mentally, I measured the distance to the glove box and how fast I could snap open the door, if I distracted him for a moment. I kept the car going with the traffic, ready to pull up next to a police car, a Highway Patrol trooper, or crash the car into the retaining wall. I had no way of warning Cat.

My thoughts were interconnected nightmares. Lane. Stacy. Jackels. Cat. Escape. The man who attacked me at the fence. I couldn't describe features to police because his face was covered. In the mirror, I dared to check on Cat. The knife was riding close to her neck. Poplin took his free hand

and pulled the mesh down from his face. When I could, I kept checking the mirror. His eyes flicked from side to side, never settling on one place. Poplin's jaw pumped up and down, working on the gum.

I kept my voice as calm as I could. "You were very clever to pin this on someone else." The exit for US 27 was two miles away.

A smile seared across his face.

"The mask isn't to conceal my face. It's use is for my work. I have to keep the contact to a minimum."

I understood the garb. The gloves. The mask. Poplin sealed himself up, eliminating the person-to-person exchange of body fibers during the murders. The less chance of giving up *his* DNA. I had him talking.

"You used Greg Wilding's DNA, didn't you? How did you do it? Let me guess. The so-called burglaries at Greg's flop house."

"Keep guessing and driving," Wilding said.

"You took his hairbrush."

"I have a question for you, Mr. Bowens. How could Greg Wilding explain to police how his hair fibers got under the nails of the victims? A convicted stalker? With so much attention on DNA . . ." Poplin laughed. High pitched, and yet restless.

"How did you two meet?"

Poplin's look became more serious. He didn't say anything until I turned off the interstate due north on US 27, headed straight for the brush fires. His arm looked tired and he readjusted the knife. He turned his stare directly into Cat's face.

"We're almost ready for me to do my work. I warn you. Don't say anything."

"Leave her alone!" The car rolled to the right. I guided the steering wheel back and got the car centered in the lane.

"Just drive!" When he yelled, he jerked his body forward and his jacket opened. In the mirror, I could see what appeared to be the tips of forceps. A row of them all neat and secure in sealed plastic and tucked into sewn pockets. That's how he planted the hair. It would be simple to pull the hair from the brush and work the strands into the nails. The mesh netting covered his chest. I let the seconds and minutes pass.

"How did you meet Wilding?" I got his attention back on me.

"How does anyone meet an alcoholic? At a bar. I'm sure he doesn't remember it. But I remember him." The smile returned to Poplin's face. "I watched Greg." Poplin seemed to like the question. "I watched him follow Anita Fulton. I learned from him."

We passed an emergency call box. One is located every few miles. Stranded motorists only had to pick up the phone and emergency help was on the other line. I smelled the smoke. The whir of television helicopters were above us. The choppers stayed in one central area, near the line of brush fires along US 27.

"We're close." Poplin pushed up closer to Cat.

"Why Cat? Let her go—"

"Shut up."

The traffic slowed. Two highway patrol troopers were working with a forestry division crew. They were looking at a map and not at the drab gray cab rolling past them. The smell of burned wood filled the car. Cat let out a cough. Behind me in the mirror, a highway patrol trooper held up his hands to the line of cars. The road was being shut down. Just get his attention. A look his way. A nod. Ahead, black fingers of smoke stretched across the highway. On my left, patches of fire churned sawgrass and marsh brush into a roaring blaze. The low breeze stoked the flames, burning hammocks and long-stemmed weeds of goldenrod, cooking the brush down to the muck.

One last chance to get the trooper's attention.

Poplin put his hand over Cat's mouth.

The trooper turned away. We kept going a half-mile.

"Slow down," Poplin ordered.

The fire trucks were behind us. I eased the speed back. The distance between the bogus cab and other drivers was becoming larger. Soon, we were the only car in the area.

Again, I gauged the distance to the glove box. I only needed a second. If I could get him laughing again. Remove his focus off Cat and maybe I could find something to go at his eyes.

"Why are you doing this?" I asked.

I felt Poplin's stare on my neck. I prepared for a thrust of the knife.

"The people on the summit committee."

"Why them?"

"They didn't understand my work." I watched Poplin in the mirror. His gaze was fixed on the fires. "They gave the public relations job to someone else. Months ago. I followed Lane home one night to convince her to change her mind. That was supposed to be my job. I wanted to work with Lane." He licked the top of his bottom lip, his chewing now slowed to a calm pace, the reflection of brush fires burned into his dark eyes. "I liked following her. When she wouldn't change her mind, I knew she had to be made to understand."

"And Stacy too?" I whispered.

"Why stop?" His gaze now appeared to focus on the road ahead. "Stop. Right over there." Poplin pointed to a spot in the highway where the road shoulder widened and allowed more room for someone to fix a flat tire.

There would have to be a chance when he forced Cat out of the car. Or would he act while in the back seat? He could dump a body and keep going.

"Get out," he ordered.

I didn't move. I waited for Poplin to open his door first. Wait. I wanted him to take his eyes off Cat. Just once.

"Get out!"

Poplin set the knife in a new position, putting the blade on the left side of her neck.

"Out!" he yelled.

I started out the door. The handle clicked open. I glanced at Poplin. He started to pull Cat toward his left.

NOW.

I reached across the length of the seat. Just one quick motion to open the glove box. The small door popped and dropped down. There was no weapon. No screwdriver. But two things fell to the floorboard. The sight of them made me stop.

A shoe and a bracelet.

I had to get away from them. My fingers curled into a tight fist.

"I kept something for myself." Poplin and Cat stood outside the car. He wrestled out of his jacket and tossed it into the cab, switching the knife from one hand to the other. Then he re-gripped his left hand around Cat's throat. The knife rested against her skin, the blade flashing red and yellow glints. I couldn't see her eyes, but I saw her tremble.

Poplin smiled. "Lane's shoe, and Stacy's bracelet. Trophies."

His jaw kept pumping, working on the gum.

I stepped out of the car. Slow. I wanted to survey the area. Behind him, the fires channeled the smoke like stovepipes. The heat warmed the side of my clothes. We were close enough to hear the crackle.

"You first, Matt. Over there. It's time to end this."

Chapter Forty-six

Poplin pointed his knife tip toward a small clearing next to the water. The fires of the Everglades raged around us. A row of melaleuca trees turned crimson. Flames leaped from a spread of fiery branches to nearby tree trunks. Poplin's baseball cap was pushed back on his head.

"Stop there," he said.

The flying embers spread into the air. He made us stop near the edge of the water. Small circles broke the surface. A fish swam away from the bank.

"Stop!" Cat yelled. The heavy smoke made her cough.

"Nothing can stop this. Lane couldn't stop it. Stacy was easy. Lane ignored me."

"You can let us go," Cat pleaded.

Poplin pushed her face toward the flame coming off a tree. I moved in closer. Cat drove her right foot into his leg and tried to duck away from the blade. She broke free from his grasp. I closed my fist and drove all my weight behind the punch, landing hard into his chest. My left arm swung at his knife hand and caught his wrist. The knife tip inched down closer to my face. I pushed back, to keep the blade at a distance. The muscles in his neck drew tight.

I took in a breath and shoved him hard, forcing him backward. Poplin waved the knife toward my midsection and stepped toward me.

"It was easy." His eyes moved from me to Cat. "Lane and

208

Stacy . . . they even dressed for me." He took another step. Poplin lunged and ripped a line through the smoky air in front of me with his knife. I jumped back. The blade cut a line through my shirt, just missing skin.

"An important meeting . . . that's what I told them." He shifted the knife from his right hand to his left and back to his right. "When they found their car was out of service. Someone was right there to offer a ride." Poplin's grin turned up one side of his face.

I reached down to my right and grabbed a burning stick. One end was still cool to the touch. I jabbed the stick at Poplin's smile and missed his face. Again. He stepped back. I waved the branch back and forth. His right foot slipped on the bank and into the water. When he tried to lift his boot, he slipped again. I aimed the branch at his midsection and thrust. Poplin dropped the knife as he crashed backward into the black pool of water. He drove his hands down into the water, splashing with his arms.

Poplin never had a chance to stand up. His eyes bulged and he grabbed at his back. Small waves rolled toward us until they hit the bank. His face contorted as if a spear went through him. He slapped a hand on his neck and let out a scream. A pattern of bent angles formed in the water and a snake eased between Poplin's legs, until the cottonmouth dropped into the shallows.

The knife remained on the bank.

"I think I can get him out." I got ready to jump into the water. Poplin's body stretched out, a floating figure moving away from me. The poison coursed through him.

"Stop fighting it. Let me help you," I yelled.

We only had minutes to get him to a hospital. I positioned myself on the bank but stopped when I saw the slow movement in the water. Only bubbles at first, then the head of the gator surfaced, showing moist black eyes, and a wide snout. The water rippled somewhere behind his tail. The alligator was probably twelve feet long.

Cat took my arm and held me back. "Don't try it."

Poplin's moans carried with the wind and the sizzle of

burned sap and the rows of cattails turning to ash. His body drifted away from me.

The gator remained fixed as if content to let Poplin come to him. The snout bumped Poplin's right shoulder, the way a hunter lined up the target in the cross hairs. The jaw opened and took Poplin by the head, snapping his body under the water. The gator spun downward, rolling over, kicking up a spray with each turn. Poplin's arms flopped limp to his side. They both went under. And then there was nothing.

I held my hand out to Cat. She ignored my reach and wrapped her arms around my body, pulling me in tight. Her head rested against my chest.

"C'mon," she whispered. "Let's go."

Chapter Forty-seven

T wo wildlife officers and a member of the medical examiner's office aboard an airboat, pulled the remains of Wayne Poplin from the Everglades. I remember airboat captains telling me a gator probably wouldn't bother a man standing on the bank. We appear to be too big to eat. But if you get down in the water, flat on your back, like Poplin, you lost your advantage. The heavy splash alone might trigger a strike.

The fires wore on, but rain was in the forecast. Cat was taken home by two uniforms and a crisis counselor. It was almost 10 P.M. when I reached the bureau.

I realized the first time I saw Poplin with Stacy, he was probably trying to convince her to reconsider the decision and hire him.

Detective Collins was waiting for me when I entered the bureau. "Ike let me in," Collins offered. "You okay?"

I dropped into the chair and leaned back against my desk. "I'm fine."

Collins stood there with a detective's patience. "We were worried about you."

"I just keep thinking, the day I saw Poplin talking with Stacy, he was probably trying to get the PR job. I just never figured . . ."

Collins pulled out a sheet of paper. "We searched Poplin's office. In a closet we found pictures taken of Lane

211

Redmond's house and photographs he must have taken of her leaving the office, going home, that sort of thing." Collins ran his finger down the page as if he didn't want to miss something. "And yes, we found paperwork that must have come from Stacy's briefcase. It was an unfavorable review of his PR firm."

"Didn't he realize if he took something from her car, the review was probably in a computer somewhere?" I checked my stomach where the knife blade tore my shirt.

"Poplin desperately needed the work." Collins dropped the paper inside a folder. "We checked with the Chamber of Commerce. He was fired from one PR firm, and other businesses were not hiring him. He was on the verge of bankruptcy."

"You did get a phone call from the jail." Mike Brendon stepped around his desk, moving into the middle of the room. "Wilding called collect. He said to say thank you."

I turned to Detective Collins. "What's his status?"

"He's got a court appearance tomorrow," Collins said. "Right now, the only thing he's facing is the parole violation. And after all this, I'm sure the judge will set up some kind of program to let him out." Collins paused. "I wasn't sure you were giving us much credit."

"Credit?"

"Just because we wanted to talk with Wilding, it didn't mean he was guilty. In his stalking case, a judge granted us permission to take his hair samples. They were a perfect DNA match for Wilding but it was too easy. Too simple."

"So you figured someone planted his hair at the scene?"

"After the burglaries of his hairbrush, it seemed to fit. Wilding was set up but we didn't have all the facts."

"So why arrest Wilding?"

"We wanted him off the street to look into this."

"And Poplin is responsible for all three murders?"

Collins pointed to the TV. Our attention shifted to the bank of televisions on the wall. Senator Priscomb was giving a statement on Channel 14. We turned and watched the television. Brendon pumped up the volume.

Priscomb said, "I just want to thank the police department for all their help in bringing this matter to a close. My wife is still in Tallahassee, but I spoke to her and she is getting better each day as we both deal with this tragedy in our lives. And we feel for the families of these three fine people."

Detective Collins again pointed to the television. "That was videotape. That's another reason why I stopped by. The real thing is coming up."

"What is he talking about?" I asked Brendon.

"They didn't want me to say anything until it was confirmed, and the police and the station wanted to wait until your debriefing was over."

"Wait for what?"

"For this." Detective Collins reached for the remote control and increased the volume of the television. On the screen, we watched Lankin standing outside the pillbox talking to the camera:

"That statement from Senator Priscomb was made just thirty minutes ago. But police are now confirming that Senator John Priscomb, the man who once headed up the subcommittee on counterfeiting is now being charged with murder."

I moved closer to the television. I watched as Lankin looked over his shoulder then turned back to the camera.

"Senator Priscomb is being charged with the murder of William Jackels, who spearheaded the committee to host a summit on counterfeit money. And the senator is also being charged with the murder of indicted counterfeiter Hector Colon who was found shot to death. And we—"

Lankin turned to a police car pulling into the parking lot.

"There's Senator Priscomb now. I'm going to move in, if I can, for a question."

Cameras, still photographers, and reporters all meshed into a body of moving arms and legs. Microphones were thrust at the face of Senator Priscomb. A uniform escorted him from the car and toward the front door of the pillbox.

"Can you explain your involvement, Senator?" Lankin yelled at the man in handcuffs. I could make out the voice of

Sandra Capers. "What about the money, Senator, was it for the money?"

Priscomb walked head down, and fast. The time in front of the cameras was perhaps twenty seconds.

Again the camera focused on Lankin. "No response from the senator," he said. "No response on the allegations he killed Jackels and Colon, the man police now say was starting to cooperate with the government. There's also the question of the money. Federal sources are now telling us Senator Priscomb has been receiving bribe money for years to tip off Colon about federal investigations."

Collins lowered the volume. "The feds are really interested in Priscomb."

"Michael Ivory?" I asked.

"We'll announce at a news conference that Jackels was responsible for flipping Hector Colon. Jackels had a final meeting in the park. He always wore jogging clothes."

"Jackels convinced Colon to testify?" I was ready to reach for my reporter pad, then stopped.

"The feds were building a case against Priscomb. They'll say Priscomb found out about Jackels and Colon. I'm just giving you a heads up. Ivory will give you all the details."

I thought about what Collins was telling me. Senator Priscomb used his daughter's death to cover up his own handiwork. Police never mentioned a DNA tie to the death of Jackels because there wasn't any.

"And the counterfeit money?" I checked the clock. Forty minutes until news time.

"The fake money was a slap at the case and at Jackels." Collins stepped toward the door. "Priscomb never planned to go to Tallahassee until much later. He had a driver take his wife up, except the driver went through the toll booth without paying. A surveillance camera caught him and the tag. You can see the driver in the picture, along with Mrs. Priscomb. But no senator. He wasn't in the car."

"He was here paying a visit on Jackels," I said.

"Take care of your friend," Collins said.

"Cat? Thanks."

Chapter Fofty-eight

"Look Matt. Snow!" Jason Miller aimed a finger at the branches of a Royal Poinciana tree.

"Snow? What do you know about snow?" I picked up Jason and placed him on my shoulders. "You've never seen snow in your life."

"Yes I have," said the voice above my head.

"I don't know what he's talking about." Cat shook her head.

Channel 14 gave me a week off to rest. No phone calls or special reports. Lankin covered the news conference with Michael Ivory. Jerry Redmond took Skids back to Atlanta. Cat received two weeks away from her job at the bank and took time off from school. We strolled down Las Olas Boulevard, taking in the shops. Cat stopped. "You know, there was that time when my mother took them for a week. They might have seen snow on a trip."

"We did Ma, you just don't remember," Shauna added. She used her hands to pull her hair back from the wind.

"Oh, yeah. I think the kids were in Georgia," Cat said. "That was the year of the freak storm." Her eyes flashed a brown brilliance.

Jason again raised a finger at the tree.

"You see. Snow!"

We looked up. Dozens of egrets lined every branch. The birds rested at attention, jammed together beak to tail. Their blanched white feathers hid the branches. Nothing could be seen except the rows of plumage. They sat there comfortably basking in the serenity of a northern breeze. Until a four-year-old cupped his hands to yell.

11/05